To KAREN - THANK YOU FOR Xmas 2020 GIVING ME A BEAUTIFUL DAUGHTER! IT WAS FUN TO WATCH NICK + HOLLY GROW UP AS WELL. ENJOY YOUR READ. LOVE YA!

SEMPER Fi
DOUG

# HEART SHOTS

## A VIETNAM WAR VETERAN'S TROUBLED HEART

To Karen ♡ from my to yours ♡ !
II Cor 1:8
II Tim 2: 11-12
We have all had "Heart Shots" in our lives. If you have, I hope this book provides comfort & healing too you as you journey through its pages

### BY DR. BOB LANTRIP

Dr Bob Lantrip

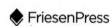 FriesenPress

Suite 300 - 990 Fort St
Victoria, BC, V8V 3K2
Canada

www.friesenpress.com

ISBN
978-1-5255-7477-1 (Hardcover)
978-1-5255-7478-8 (Paperback)
978-1-5255-7479-5 (eBook)

*Fiction, War & Military*

Distributed to the trade by The Ingram Book Company

# Table of Contents

# Dedication

*I would like to dedicate this book to the following people!*

*My Wife of 51 years Delva Nadine Lantrip, who has stuck by me during the times of uncertainty and trials. A woman who knows what "Semper Fidelis" really means.*

*My Mother, the late Florence Yvonne Lantrip who prayed two combat Veterans through the Vietnam War.*

*To Doug Witcraft, Squad leader and all members of 1st Squad 1st Platoon, Hotel Company, 2nd Battalion, 26th Marine Regiment.*

*To the surviving members of Marine Corps Boot Camp Platoon 3041,*

*"The Boys from Washington."*

*And lastly to those who did not return from the war, their lives were cut short.*
*We will never forget you!*

# Preface

WHO CAN KNOW how life flows? This short **novel** was written by a Vietnam veteran years after the war. As he journeyed from home to war, his future was uncertain. **Heart Shots** is a book about life, death, and the uncertainty of life. How does one measure the experiences of life?

As you journey through these pages, may your heart be challenged by the events that unfold. Perhaps you have questions about your own life? Why did certain things happen, why did you go through tragedy, and what was the good in it? Walk with me as we journey together. Perhaps you will see my heart. And perhaps you will see your heart … and get a glimpse of a heart that has been shot!

Many men die from bullets, some die from words. How will the Marine, Damon Lee Lane, fare as his life is stretched to the breaking point. Will the shot through the heart take his life? Will his family ever be the same?

Let us journey together.
Dr. Bob Lantrip

# Introduction

SOUND ASLEEP AFTER an exhausting day at work, Daniel Albert Lane jolted awake when his front doorbell shattered the silence like the ringing of Big Ben in London. An eerie feeling settled around him as the ringing stopped and silence once again engulfed the night. He knew something was wrong.

Shakily peering out his bedroom window to the driveway below, he noticed the fresh coat of snow that had fallen since he'd drifted off to sleep. Tire tracks in the street below made a curving path into his driveway. Below, a black official-looking vehicle waited, its lights still on and the engine running.

Daniel's heart sank as he tried to reason what was about to unfold. A sickening feeling grasped his soul, and he broke into a sweat of terror he hadn't experienced since the beaches of Iwo Jima during WWII. He didn't want to open the door. A vehicle like that meant bad news awaited him. His son. Damon, was in Vietnam, and in harm's way.

Daniel stumbled toward the door, shocked, and afraid.

As he opened the front door, a Marine Corps officer and a Navy chaplain greeted him with solemn looks. "Are you Daniel Albert Lane, father of Marine Lance Corporal Damon Lee Lane?" the officer asked.

"Yes." Daniel's throat and chest tightened with each waiting second.

The young officer spoke plainly. "Sir, I regret to inform you that on May 15th in the Quang Nam Province of South Vietnam, during Operation

Taylor Common, your son, Lance Corporal Damon Lee Lane, was killed in action from enemy fire.

"Damon was shot through the heart and died instantly. He was assaulting an enemy position and destroyed it, saving the lives of his fellow Marines, just before receiving a fatal rifle shot from a sniper hidden above the enemy position. The report said he did not suffer."

"Sir," said the chaplain, "there will be a service officer in contact with you within 24 hours to assist you in returning the body of your son to you. They will also help you with any matters pertaining to this event and answer any further questions you might have. We are sorry for your loss."

With that, the officers were gone, and Daniel stood alone, in the dark, numb and miserable!

Daniel wished he had said more to the officers, even though their news had been devastating. Not certain what to do next, he collapsed in disbelief onto the living room couch. How would he tell his wife Yvonne? He was clueless as to how he'd make it up the staircase to where she was so soundly sleeping, without a care in the world. All he could do was lay his head back on the couch and let his paralyzed legs and emotions rest just for a minute. He prayed for strength, sleep, and a miracle.

"Daniel! Daniel!" The voice penetrated deep into Daniel's soul. "Wake up. Wake up, honey. You're having another nightmare."

Daniel jerked awake; sweat drenched his body and the bedsheets. His pillow lay beneath him, sopping wet. Fear gripped Daniel's heart as he tried to understand what was happening.

"It was Damon, Yvonne," Daniel said, talking fast. "It was Damon," Daniel rattled on while Yvonne tried to figure out what he was talking about. "Marine officers called on us to tell us he is dead. He was killed, shot through the heart in Vietnam."

Yvonne drew back in disbelief. "Daniel, you were dreaming. There were no officers here. You're scaring me. Stop it!"

"A dream? No officers? No message from Vietnam?" Daniel swung his feet to the bedroom floor and sat with his head bowed in his hands as tears gave release from the stress. He questioned his own sanity. It had all seemed so real. "Please, God," he cried out, "keep my son Damon safe, in Vietnam."

# Introduction Heart Shot

*The heart shots at the end of every chapter are from the heart of Damon Lee Lane, a man who experienced the toughness of military life. Each heart shot explains what is happening inside Damon as he travels from a peaceful life to one ravaged by war. Damon has already heard about the knocks on the doors of military families, knocks that deliver bad news. He already knows one of the greatest fears of parents and spouses is the news that their loved ones are never coming home.*

*Will he be one of them?*

# Chapter One

## *Before the Corps*

DAMON LEE LANE was born the cold winter morning of October 8, 1949. The old house in Yakima, WA, wasn't much more than a couple of cabins nailed together. That house still stands today, quietly lingering even after many additions and remodels. Damon was born with a medical condition that required an immediate blood transfusion. He had a type of hematoma that needed to be removed before he could be discharged from the hospital. He also was anemic and would need a blood transfusion after the surgery.

Damon's dad, Daniel, said, "The only person who had volunteered to give him blood for the transfusion was a colored man." So, the standard joke was that Damon was part colored. That didn't bother Damon at all and he would realize soon enough that all men bled red.

Damon was raised with a caring mother and father, two older brothers and two younger sisters. Yep, an absolute middle child. Other than that, his childhood ran rather smoothly—school, mandatory church attendance, and an extreme shyness that seemed to hold him back. Damon hung around with several of his high school buddies and often frequented an old skating rink in town, if nothing else because they let you skate as fast as you wanted during the fast sessions.

During one of these trips to Skateland, Damon met *her*. His guys had stopped by a couple of gals and were giving them a bad time until Damon saw her. Her name was Christina Deguyer—young, very pretty, and petite, with long brown hair and a peaceful spirit that was enough to calm anybody who ran with a gang of boys like Damon's. Damon was too young and immature to figure out that the soft sweet spirit Christina exhibited was what attracted him to her more than anything else.

The next week, she returned to Skateland and was presently surprised that her new friend had returned also. As time wore on, Christina and Damon drew close, but not close enough to know what their future together would be.

After graduation from Eisenhower Senior High School, Damon held down several jobs, which included harvesting fruit in the lush Yakima Valley. Damon thought it odd that many of his friends were one year behind him in high school. After a few classes in college, which didn't really go well, Damon realized that he was less mature than the guys in his High School Class and he was also the same age of his friends one year behind him.

After they had all graduated from high school, Damon and his two best friends decided to volunteer for military service. The Marines, of course, had the most impressive uniforms with shiny gold buttons, deep blue dress blue jacket, and light blue trousers with a blood-red stripe down each side, called a blood stripe. The blood stripe should have given him a clue of what was about to befall him, but it went unnoticed.

Thus, it was decided. He was in, enlisted into the United States Marine Corps with its 120-day delay program. It was a two-year commitment with a four-year reserve time. A total of 80 men from Washington State joined and formed the Evergreen State Platoon. In less than three months' time, these young men—boys, really—would set off to the Marine Corps Recruit Depot in San Diego, CA.

The only mistake Damon made during this time was that he didn't discuss his plans with Christina until he was enlisted. Yet, in his heart, Damon knew Christina was the one for him, so he worked fervently to buy her an engagement ring before he was called to active duty.

What the boys didn't know, and couldn't know at the time, was that this wonderful two-year program meant two things. One, it meant you had 120 days to get your things in order to prepare yourself for what lay ahead. This was an impossible task, because words alone could never describe what was ahead for these naive young recruits.

Second, it meant boot camp training (a hell of its own), infantry training, jungle warfare training, 30 days leave, then straight to a land far far away. Vietnam! Vietnam was a relatively unknown country at the time, but South Vietnam was a small country that had the ability to change a man's life forever.

It had been said, "Nothing prepares you in life for swallowing your first raw oyster." Damon had never experienced the raw-oyster effect, but he was about to find out that nothing anyone could have said or done could have prepared him for the world he was about to enter: the United States Marine Corps boot camp.

## Heart Shot One

*Damon Lee Lane was about to cross the threshold of a world in which he had before never trodden. It was a world where severe change took place, a world where new experiences took the place of what was known and familiar. Damon was introduced to homesickness, and in this instance, there was nothing he could do to change it. When it was quiet, Damon mostly reflected about the family he had left. What were they doing? What was his fiancée Christina doing? He began to realize the value of family and the hard work of his parents to maintain this thing called family. Would he ever see them again?*

*During this time, Damon appreciated letters from home and he began to realize that communication with his family was absolutely necessary.*

# Chapter Two

## *Welcome to Marine Corps Boot Camp*

PRIVATE YAKAMOTO HAD been the first person to inform everyone on the plane ride to San Diego about the calamities that were soon to befall them. Pvt Yakamoto, who was nicknamed "Yako," was the first who seemed to know what boot camp was going to be like. He also was the funniest person they had ever known. He repeatedly reported how the DIs were going to smack them around, slap them, cuss them out, and make all of them feel like they were absolutely worthless. And that would be just before breakfast! He also let them know the yelling, screaming, and physical training would be from sunup to sundown. Pvt Yako sure had a way of making them feel good about the choices they had made.

It had grown dark at the San Diego Airport. As the 80 men from Washington disembarked the jumbo jet and onto the tarmac, an uneasy quietness consumed them. Damon reasoned that they would get a good night's sleep, then start training the following day. Wrong!

There, standing by a green bus, was a giant of a man. He was tall, black, and had the biggest arms of anyone they had ever seen. He began yelling obscenities at the men, half yelling, half growling, which began a state of confusion and disorientation they would experience past the time the next ray of sunlight split the sky.

The yelling continued as the bus worked its way through the back gate of the Marine Corps Recruit Depot. What happened to the grand entrance? Where was the Marine Corps band to welcome them with pomp and circumstance? Wasn't there going to be a parade? All thoughts of glory, Marine pride, and honor had been reduced to a program of breaking down what these men thought they were and preparing them for what was yet to come. In other words, the men were totally unprepared for the hell that was about to overtake them! They knew that they were in deep trouble— and they had only met their bus driver so far.

As the bus lumbered to a crawl outside of what was known as the receiving barracks, Damon noticed three drill instructors (DIs) waiting for them. It all too soon became clear that these three men's mission for the next ten very long weeks was to make these recruits' lives as miserable as possible.

As the green bus screeched to a halt, the flash of a brown DI uniform flew through the bus. The DI yelled and screamed very colorful metaphors that actually meant, "Get your ass off my bus, you lousy maggots." All the recruits responded with an explosion of energy, trying to exit the bus as ordered and not be singled out for any "special treatment."

On the famous Marine Corps Recruit yellow footprints, the first tool used to organize new troops, Pvt Damon was right behind Pvt Yako, the company clown. By now, each recruit was more than a little rattled about the events quickly taking place. Most had never been under discipline, much less such harsh discipline, with DIs screaming in their ears.

Up front, Pvt Damon had spotted two DIs working over a tall guy. His only offense might have been being the tallest man in the platoon. Or perhaps he did not have one foot perfectly aligned over the yellow footprints painted on the asphalt waiting area. Within seconds, two DIs had this tall man down on his knees while they gave him some special corrective attention that said every detail in the Marine Corps matters! The lesson was learned, not just by the tall man, but all of them.

With the attention all on the tall guy, Pvt Yako turned his head to the private on his right and joyfully explained, "See, I told you. They gonna smack us around. Gonna get real tough!" Pvt Damon observed a flash of brown somewhere to his left and coming from behind at lightning speed.

A third DI was hidden somewhere in the back of the platoon. He had seen movement and heard words from a rebellious private. In one second, he smacked Pvt Yako upside the head, then yelled and screamed at him for what seemed like hours. His offense was unauthorized movement, talking, and making his own decisions. It appeared Pvt Yako had received some of his own medicine that night. As scary as that encounter with that sergeant was, it did not dim Pvt Yako's spirit or his sense of humor.

After the DIs got the platoon squared away, the next step was for the recruits to receive haircuts so they would all be uniform. Each man was placed in the barber's chair, then his head was shaved to the scalp. No trim, no style just a rapid shave that took about 45 seconds per man. Men looked different when their hair was gone! Which perhaps was the point, but it took Pvt Damon two whole days to recognize the two men with whom he had joined the Corps.

The next stop was the receiving barracks where the men were to take everything civilian, including all clothing, and put it in a box to be mailed home. They were given only a few seconds to get out of the horrible, slimy, civilian puke clothes and get them into a box. Pvt Damon, sensing the urgency and intensity of the moment, was having trouble unbuttoning his white shirt, so with one quick pull, the buttons popped off, and he was released from the burden of messing around with them. He reasoned that his mother would not be able to figure out what happened to the shirt once it was sent home.

By now, the night had grown old. However, the saga would continue well into the wee morning hours. The DIs taught them how to march in step to the tent area where they would spend the first few weeks. That must have been a sight, a new platoon trying to stay in step when they really hadn't even marched before. Uniforms were issued, blankets, towels, sheets for the bed, and pillowcases and a pillow along with the training on how to properly put the pillow in the pillowcase. There was only one way to make

7

their beds, the Marine Corps way, and everyone's had to be the same. The covering blanket had to be tight; no wrinkles or any hint of non-conformity was allowed. After a few more harassing comments, sometime around 3 a.m., Platoon 3041 was put to bed.

Pvt Damon pulled back the side tent flap to observe the outside area. The senior drill instructor stood at attention, on the parade deck, tall, alone but with piercing eyes. He was looking for anyone who dared just for the fun of it to violate the order to shut up, go to sleep, and not look around. At last, sleep settled in as Pvt Damon wondered what would have happened if he had been caught peering out of the tent that awful and terrible morning. Sleep settled in, and all was well.

A scream penetrated the darkness and ended any hope of just a little more sleep. "Platoon 3041, lights on and hatches open," yelled the duty DI. This was followed a minute later with, "Platoon 3041, on the road." This meant get your rack made, get dressed, and fall in formation, all in about two minutes' time.

Pvt Damon noticed one guy was still in his rack sound asleep. Before anyone else could try to wake the sleeping private, there was a flash of brown as several DIs rushed in, grabbed the private by the throat, and pulled him out of his rack, flipping the rack and its contents onto the wooden floor of the tent below. Of course, no amount of yelling and cussing at the private could have possibly been enough!

All this was happening because the boys were being taught discipline. They learned how to take care of their gear and how to maintain discipline in the midst of chaos. The physical part of boot camp really wasn't that hard, but the mental and emotional strain could take its toll on anyone who was undisciplined, weak, or just didn't want to pay the price to become a Marine.

Damon Lee Lane was a quiet sort of a person, shy and quite introverted because of his melancholy personality. He soaked in the training, learned discipline, and wondered why he, with his personality, had decided to join the Marines when most other recruits were outgoing and aggressive.

At times, discipline meant standing on a hot drill field at attention for hours. During these times, you dared not scratch your nose or swat a pesky fly because any unauthorized movement would bring the wrath of the DIs down upon you like a wild gorilla out of control. And amid the yelling and physical discipline, Damon soaked it all in, knowing there had to be a reason.

The training also consisted of weapons use and hours on the firing line with rifle and pistol. They learned how to throw hand grenades, use rocket launchers, and how to deploy claymore mines that could wipe out a whole platoon of enemy soldiers. They were also trained in hand-to-hand combat, and the DIs told them the best rush they would ever get is taking out an enemy with their bare hands or their K-Bar, the word used for the Marine fighting knife. The training and discipline were well received and, as hard as it was, the boys from Washington were being turned into lean, mean, fighting machines.

Deep in the recesses of his heart, Damon closely held the actions and disciplines of his DIs. Nobody cared for such harsh treatment, but the realization that they were being prepared for surviving something much harsher than this was slowly settling in. The training molded them into men able to survive against all odds, when the pressures of combat became all too real. And just once in a while, Damon caught a glimpse, however hidden it was, that these hard Marine DIs had a speck of humanity about them, a sense of caring, a sense that perhaps they really believed the motto, "The more you sweat in peace, the less you bleed in war."

It all began to make sense. Pvt Damon threw every ounce of his energy into learning, soaking in the disciplines, and grasping at every hint of survival of what was to come. This was also the view of Gunnery Sergeant Rocky Gallant, the toughest Marine out there; he was considered a Marine's Marine! He was their senior drill Instructor, and was a tough guy, physically as well as in the spirit of the Corps. This man took excellence personally, and he expected the same from his men. "Use the principles, and you may survive in battle and live on to fight again," he would often say. Pvt Damon prayed it was true, and hung onto every word.

Graduation day finally came, and these worthless slimy-puke boys had been turned into Marines. They hadn't been Marines when they signed up to join. They became Marines on graduation day and were called Marines for the first time that day. That day, Damon Lee and 74 other men became Marines. They entered a brotherhood, a brotherhood that would last a lifetime. And they would learn even more the motto, *Semper Fidelis*, that would live and burn within their hearts.

## *Heart Shot Two*

*The psychological impact of Marine boot camp was over. Infantry training further advanced the idea that something was looming ahead. The forced marches, weapons training, and jungle warfare training instilled in the new Marines that they needed to be ready. The uncertainty of the future would give way to the adrenaline rush of 12 to 13 months of combat in the jungles of Vietnam.*

*Now these men, unbeknown to them, had a clock running within their hearts. Uncertainty and a new enemy ... adrenaline. The Marines had an arsenal of weapons ready and waiting. Mentally, physically, and psychologically ready, with enough combat gear, which was designed to protect everything but their hearts.*

# Chapter Three

## *Preparing for War*

AFTER BOOT CAMP, the Marines were sent to Camp Pendleton, CA, to receive specialty training in their Military Occupation Status (MOS). Most became infantry men (0311), but some became machine gunners, mortar men, or door gunners on helicopters. Some went to radio School or Vietnamese language school. Whichever secondary MOS the men were trained in, all Marines were basically 0311, a Marine skilled in combat and prepared to fight in any capacity needed.

Infantry Training School was the intense part of physical training, such as climbing a mountain called Old Smokey, which was accomplished on a forced march right up the side of the mountain. No stops, no breaks, and any Marine that fell out was in an instant world of hurt! In boot camp, the men were told to obey any order without questioning. In their ITR, they learned how to do things they were ordered to do.

One amazing benefit of ITR was that once they were in the chow hall, they could take their time eating and not have to stuff the meal down in one to two minutes as they had in boot camp. The jungle warfare part of ITR trained the men in jungle settings to spot enemies who could pop up from anywhere, and to watch for and find booby traps that could kill and injure without warning. Pvt Damon honed these skills because he was in the mindset of surviving Vietnam, the black cloud of war that was looming over his head.

ITR was very physical, and it stretched Marines to their limit. One of the limit-stretchers was the gas chamber, where Marines were told to put on their gas masks before entering a building out in the training field, isolated from any other structures. Once inside, they were told that gas was going to be pumped into the building and they were to follow orders strictly! This was nothing new to these Marines. After they could see the haze of the gas filling the room, they were told to take off their masks and stay in the room until they were instructed to leave. If they panicked and left early, they would have to go back in. When they took off their masks, many tried not to breathe, but sooner or later, they had to inhale.

What happened next was totally indescribable unless one had experienced it themselves. Their eyes began to burn, their throat and nose caught fire, or at least it felt that way. Gagging and lack of proper breathing would certainly entertain the idea of panic, but the Marines just took it. When the door opened and they all hurried outside, mucous, tears, snot, and anything else that had been saturated in their sinuses over the past two weeks came out. It was a mess! But they learned that day what tear gas did to the human body and that it could render men useless in trying to resist exiting a bunker or building.

The last, most notable experience Pvt Damon had was after the Marines hiked into the training area somewhere high in the California mountains. There were bleachers set up to finalize what training had been accomplished that day.

At the end of the talk that afternoon, a new instructor got up and addressed the Marines. He said, "Up until now your training has been easy! I have you all day tomorrow and you're going to bleed, you're going to hurt, you're going to wish you had never been born! Nothing you have experienced in my Marine Corps will be worse than what is going to happen to you tomorrow!"

There was not much sleep that night. Had they not had enough already? Dread was on every man's mind, even into the night. The funny thing was, the next day, that sergeant was a good teacher, and along with the classes in the bleachers, he told them jokes, and funny ones. Part of the joke was that he had scared the crap out of the Marines and it tuned out they really liked the guy.

Damon could easily recall the jokes that had been told, but they were too raunchy to retell. Even with the jokes and classes, the men were being prepared for war. The most fun part of preparing for war was that the Marines were taught how to blow up stuff. Perhaps that gave them the sense of power they needed to survive. Yet, not all such explosive devises would function as they were supposed to.

Damon often wondered, how does one really prepare for war? Was it just in the training, like a mechanical robot following orders sent by a non-participating individual? Was it in the discipline and mental ascent given to the task? Perhaps it was in all of these. But perhaps there was more. Pvt Damon had been reasoning, in his melancholy way, that perhaps the best way to survive a war was to have a reason to—a reason to come home, a really good reason to take out the bad guys and, in reality, to protect the ones he loved at home. Damon had already been a part of a loving family. Godly parents, two older brothers and two younger sisters. Now he was engaged to Christina, and as soon as he could get his thirty days of leave, he would marry her.

Knowing he was most likely facing the Vietnam War, Damon and Christina were married November 30, 1969, in a small church in Selah, Washington, just weeks prior to his deployment to the Vietnam War. While Damon hadn't yet realized it, Christina became an anchor for him, a reason to return from a soul-crushing war that could tear the heart out of anyone. She became one of the solid rocks to moor him to the place known as home.

Damon questioned deep inside his heart, how does one survive anything? He felt another way would be to have a positive attitude that reminded him that everything would work out and a solid place to call home, a place where a man knows the connection would always be. Yet, not all the men experiencing the rigorous training and physical stress had that base to fall back upon. Damon really felt bad for the Marines he knew who had no such connections. There were some who never received letters from home, nothing.

Damon could not understand this lifestyle. No connection, no family. The question became, "Who cared for them?" What would they do when an impossible situation came up? There would be plenty of those.

## Heart Shot Three

*That one question loomed deep within Damon's soul: how does one prepare for war? Damon Lee Lane was doing everything he knew to do. Yet, there was uncertainty. Perhaps he could enlist a blind trust in someone or something that would allow everything to be okay. The strong family connections that Damon had made were sure to pay off over there, in a war-torn country, where war was not new to them. Would there still be a heart left in a man when the war would be over? What could take the place of concern, worry, and the thoughts that would not go away? Thoughts of impending doom were sure to increase the closer he got to Vietnam.*

# Chapter Four

## When It Gets Real ... Vietnam

THE PLANE RIDE into Da Nang Air Base South Vietnam was surreal. The closer they got, each man had an inward sense of dread. What lay ahead was drilling holes in the minds of each man as they searched the small strip of land below. The uncertainty of the moment added to the stress of getting closer to a combat zone. Pfc Damon Lane wondered if the ammunition so carefully accounted for in training would be so closely guarded now that they were there. Plenty of questions were forming in his mind, but one thing he knew for sure: he was now in Vietnam and was afraid his life was about to change forever.

Pfc Damon Lee Lane, who had recently been promoted, was assigned to Hotel Company, 2nd Battalion, 26th Marine Regiment. They were the Marines who took part in the decisive Battle of Khe Sanh the previous year. The stories of that heated battle would become legend in the history of the Marine Corps, as well as the rest of the world.

Hotel Company was in the field on an operation, so Pvt Damon and a few other Hotel Company replacements were flown south to Chu Lai, South Vietnam, which became known as the hell hole of Viet Cong and their booby traps. There was an overnight stay at the Chu Lai Marine Base, and the next day helicopters came in to pick up the Marines and fly them to the *USS Tripoli*, an aircraft carrier designed to disburse Marines from the flight deck deep into jungles infested with Viet Cong and North Vietnamese Regular Army Troops. Since the combat troops of Hotel Company were in the field, the new guys were outfitted with all the gear they would need when it was their time to be inserted into the jungles. Needless to say, it was a time of high anxiety, and the waiting was only made bearable because at least for now, they were still safe and alive. How long this would continue was the question in each new man's mind.

The present operation had become known to 1st Squad, 1st Platoon as Chu Lai I. That wasn't the official name, but the significance of the battles at Chu Lai demanded keeping them straight. Chu Lai was a small city south of Da Nang, which had become an infiltration point for the Viet Cong and the NVA soldiers who gave them their orders. It was also a convenient storage place to hide munitions since many of the civilians were Viet Cong sympathizers. So, the barber who cut their hair in the barber shop by day, could be the man to cut their throat after the lights went out at night. This was the way of the Viet Cong.

The battles at Chu Lai were furious. 1st Squad was sent out on a patrol that day. Leading point, the position that Damon was soon to take over, was Cpl Ramond Laramos, squad leader. Ramond had a feeling something was coming down that day, which was why he wanted to walk point. As Ramond was about halfway through the two-mile patrol, he stepped up on a rice paddy dike to get a better look at the pathway before him.

One more step down the dike and all hell broke loose. There was a terrific explosion that was loud enough to disorientate every man in the squad. Time seemed to stand still as the dust cloud enveloped Cpl Laramos. A legless body was thrown into the air and down range a few yards, landing on the elevated paddy dike. Instantly after that, machine-gun fire and AK-47 small arms fire opened up on the disorientated squad. The squad was pinned down, and all hope of getting away alive was lost.

The ambush had been perfectly planned. The Marines had walked right into it. Now they were stuck. It was a horseshoe ambush, where chaos was caused from the initial booby trap, then from three sides a hail of bullets rained in and the Marines were mostly being shot to pieces. The enemy had them right where they wanted them. Knowing Marines took care of their own and would try to help their squad leader, the enemy continued to machine-gun the body of the downed Marine. They were hoping to draw more Marines into the open and machine-gun the hell out of them!

Amidst the chaos, there arose a little sawed-off Marine they all called WOP. He was very small, short but very wiry. He was a fire team leader, which was over about three other men. Out of the chaos, WOP took charge. He organized the squad by forming a defensive position and then ordered proper return of fire to hold the enemy at bay. Once the enemy knew the squad was organized and able to fight back, they had second thoughts about their actions.

Once WOP radioed in for help, another squad was sent out to help, rushing to aid in the battle and to help bring back those who were killed or wounded. Among them was a tall, lanky, handsome young Marine they soon started to call Wild Wit. WOP told everyone later that he was scared spitless during the fight, but when he saw Wit he knew they would be alright. WOP was a young Marine from Yuma, AZ, named Cpl Gerioso. WOP earned a Bronze Star that day for his cool-headed actions, which saved lives and denied the enemy further advancement.

This was the scenario that Pfc Damon walked into and learned of, his first few days in Vietnam. Pfc Damon's platoon, in such a short period of time, had two men killed and four wounded, including the Navy corpsman who had patrolled with them, and a little Puerto Rican named Dianggelo, who was shot through the leg. The baptism of fire had taken a hard toll on the men of 1st Squad. Wild Wit was asked to take over 1st Squad as their new squad leader and help rebuild it to fighting strength. This was Wit's second tour of duty in Vietnam, so he was the most likely and experienced candidate.

Wild Wit was a great squad leader. He had received his baptism of fire in his first tour of duty in July and October 1967. He was with Golf Company, 2nd Battalion, 9th Marines up near the Demilitarized Zone (DMZ). The DMZ was supposed to be an area where no armies would cross. The North Vietnamese paid little attention to the rules and often came across anyway, then later on went around the DMZ using what had been called the Ho Chi Min Trail. The Con Thien Firebase and Marine compound where Wit's company operated from was very close to the DMZ, and patrols would often permeate the border and penetrate a little deeper into the DMZ than was allowed. Many patrols and ambushes had been carried out from the marine base because sometimes the enemy were as thick as flies and they needed to be thinned out.

The platoon that day was ordered to search inside the DMZ because of recent activity that was reported about NVA soldiers being in the zone and digging in. Wit didn't really care to go out on that day because it was cloudy, rainy, and downright miserable. A Marine has a way of knowing when trouble lies ahead, and the Marines prepared for the worst. The enemy were digging in alright! They were setting up an ambush and had purposely exposed themselves to the intelligence officers so they would send the Marines into a trap that would be very well laid out and sprung on the unsuspecting Marines.

As 2nd Platoon worked their way into the area where the NVA had been spotted, the landscape only provided one passage through. The Marines carefully took the narrow passage and soon were enveloped in an ambush site of well-hidden enemy soldiers. It was a three-sided ambush, very well planned and executed! With loud explosions and enemy fire, the ambush instantly was sprung. The gunfire seemed to be coming from everywhere.

Two men directly on the left of Wit were down; bullets whizzed through and shattered the vegetation and limbs of the trees. There was no place to hide, no way of escape, and by now the enemy was charging through the Marine's loosely laid perimeter and seeking out any Marines who still needed to be killed! The NVA's business that day was to kill as many Marines as they could, and business was good!

Wit sprang into action with his M16 right after the first two of his men went down. As he was firing and engaging in the heat of the battle, three more men went down on his right. All of a sudden, as he reloaded his M16 and emptied another magazine into an enemy running hell-bent on killing him, he felt a *zing* and a stunning feeling in his head, but he was still alive and fought on!

As quickly as it started, it was over. The Marines were hunkered down and keeping a sharp eye out in case the NVA wanted a little more blood. Wit was lying on his left side, watching carefully. He knew that things needed to settle down before there was too much movement again. The smoke and carnage seemed suspended in the air as the enemy hastily retreated to who knew where. Wit couldn't quite make out who of his men were left at this point. Was he the only one?

The gloomy, rainy, fog-infested sky seemed to change in intensity for a second. Wit, still on his side, looked up to see the fog lift and a bright, shining light coming through the opening in the clouds and surrounding his body. Did he just die? But then he noticed something that had come through the clouds and drifted down to where he was. It was a white feather that slowly floated back and forth until it came to rest near his left arm. Wit knew the battle was over and he picked up the feather as the clouds closed together, sealing the area through which the light had been coming. Wit wanted to keep the white feather, so he placed it in a New Testament that he had been carrying. He opened the pages to find a safe place for safekeeping. He noticed the place he put the feather was at II Timothy 2:11–12:

> If we died with Him,
> We shall also live with Him.
> If we endure,
> We shall also reign with him
> If we deny Him,
> He also will deny us.

Wit had a sense that there was more going on that day, and he pondered the significance of the events. But like most Marines, he put the New Testament away, and tucked his questions away, in a footlocker called his soul. Soon, more stuff would be pushed down to that place, to be sorted out later. But for now, he was alive and he planned on keeping it that way for the rest of his tour.

As the body count commenced, Wit learned that there were more than a few Marines that were killed or wounded. Fifteen of the enemy soldiers killed were counted toward Wit's quick action, his facing the enemy straight on and giving them the barrel of his M-16. Remembering the zinging feeling and his now-intense headache, Wit removed his helmet. A deep trench ran along the rim of the helmet, digging deeply into the metal before veering off into the air. This was an example of a close call, often heard of in battle. It also explained the weird sensation of a vibrating AK-47 round that almost hit its mark just a few minutes before.

This was the man who was now leading 1st Squad, 1st Platoon, two years later. A man who was tall, very experienced, not afraid to straighten you out if you did something wrong, yet underneath his tough exterior was a heart of gold. Wit led the squad with what seemed to be little effort. He was a natural leader, and that was what the squad needed more than anything.

This squad was reinforced and whipped into shape because of Wit's expertise in the world of combat. The squad became known as Wild Wit's Raiders! These Raiders were men who could slip in and out of enemy strongholds and rage utter chaos in their midst, more chaos than Chu Lai had done to them. And more often than not, they would return with all their men, safe and sound.

This was the hell into which Pfc Damon had been thrown. As the Marines returned to the ship, Damon somewhat nervously observed the condition of these battle-weary Marines. For the first time, he observed men who had experienced battle, men who had borne each other's burdens to the point of death. Damon secretly prayed that he would be worthy of their honor in the heat of the battles to come.

As the men cleared and unloaded their gear, Damon could not believe the weight these men had been carrying. He was only more surprised by the extent of the blood, sweat, mud, and jungle filth that seemed to cling to them. What had they been through? What accounted for the thousand-yard stares many of them had developed? Pfc. Lane had received some of his combat gear and thought it to be a heavy load, but nothing had prepared him for the reality of combat after being inserted into a jungle, carrying even more gear, and being cut off from humanity as he knew it.

As Damon contemplated what was developing, he began to understand: the Marines were serious about their mission. They would get the job done, no matter the cost. These men could be counted upon. They had each written a blank check to the United States of America, up to and including their life. Damon might have begun to feel a little unworthy had he not seen the extensive magnitude of stress on these men s faces. Some had a look of terror, some not so much. But he knew, it's not so much what the men were saying as it was their unspoken words. Marines have a way of transmitting information without a word. Damon would learn this, and soon. As a future point man, this skill could perhaps save lives, maybe even his. In his heart, Damon could not yet fully understand the horror of combat that his new Marine family had experienced. Yet he had the feeling that soon, very soon, he would complete the picture in his mind. Damon believed it was all about to get real!

## Heart Shot Four

*Damon had always thought his heart was a relatively tender thing. As Pfc Damon Lee Lane now prepared for the most traumatic time in his life, who cared about what was about to happen to him? His family? His friends back home? Society or the politicians who sent him there?*

*Right now, Damon is concerned. He has heard about the snipers; he has heard about the ambushes and booby traps. He has now seen the terror in the faces of his newly acquired squad. When the battle becomes real, will he survive or will he be shot through the heart and not get a chance to say goodbye?*

# Chapter Five

## *Combat Shock of Lynn River*

THE WORD CAME down, not just a rumor, that a new operation had been planned and they needed to get ready to go! Operation Lynn River would start twelve miles south of Da Nang, Vietnam. The mission was to rout out the Viet Cong strongholds and restore security to that area.

The recently returned Marines had turned in all live ammunition after coming aboard the ship. Now they were being replenished with deadly ordnance for the mission—rifle rounds, mortar rounds, extra cans of machine gun ammo, and plenty of hand grenades. Ammunition was handed out like candy in the candy store! Pfc Damon naively asked, "Why are they giving out so much ammunition?"

The reply was swift and certain. "Because we're going to need it where we're going!"

The same sinking feeling that Pfc Damon had experienced earlier not only set in again, but the dread of the moment became quite sobering. He thought, *This is what I dreaded the most, when getting real becomes deadly!*

The Marines lined up on the flight deck to board the CH-47s, double-bladed helicopters with enough capacity to carry a whole squad of Marines. Pfc Damon whispered a prayer, the best way he knew how, hoping, somewhere there was a God out there listening. As the choppers lifted off the flight deck and headed inland, Damon tightly clutched his M16. Soon the order came down to lock and load. Well, he knew what that meant!

Within minutes, it seemed, the choppers were spiraling down like pigeons do when returning to their nest. The CH-47 had this capability, which really helped the Marines get on target quickly, accurately, and without becoming more than a moving target to the enemy.

A few hundred yards before hitting the floor of the looming rice paddy below, a sharp bothersome noise caught Damon's attention. The slight *ping ping ping* seemed odd over the sounds of the engine! Looking up, above the head of Wild Wit, Damon saw two holes appear in the thin skin of the helicopter. Wit just kind of smiled and didn't flinch. How could this be? Pfc Damon later learned from Wit that it is the bullets you don't hear or see that get you. When you see or hear them fly by you, you're in great shape. This was a lesson Damon would learn all too well.

This operation was a squeeze operation. Other battalions of Marines had been deployed in different areas in a triangle fashion, with open spaces at each point of the triangle. The Marines then began the squeeze by moving their companies forward, forcing the enemy closer and closer to the center of the triangle. As the triangle compressed, the Marines stopped. The enemy was right where they wanted them.

Hotel Company, 1st Platoon choppered right into this triangle. The enemy scattered and everywhere they turned they ran into Marines. It almost didn't seem fair. Nevertheless, the enemy were denied their hiding places, their munitions storage and, in most cases, their lives.

Damon realized it was true that a Marine could be your best friend or your worst enemy. He proved himself that day in a baptism of fire that solidified his relationship with his fellow Marines through the defeat of an enemy that never had played fair. They squashed the brutal and savage attacks of the NVA and Viet Cong, and the lawlessness of the Viet Cong had been overcome. The Marines restored order to the area, but for how long?

As darkness approached, the Marines dug in. Had it not been for the wisdom of the operation's planners, the night could have belonged to the Viet Cong. All night long, illumination was provided from above. Large canisters, dropped by parachute, lit the night sky like daylight. In the distance, gunships worked over any areas where enemy troops were hiding. Damon could always tell when a new illumination canister was on its way. There would be a popping sound, a flash of new light, then a whooping sound as the cover of the illumination canister fell to the ground. It was an eerie sound, but a very welcome one. The coordination of illumination, air support, and the fact that there was a Marine awake and watching in every foxhole provided a few hours of sleep for the battle-weary Marines!

Out of nowhere, a single enemy soldier came, probing their lines, looking for a weak spot. Armed to the teeth, he slowly approached. A Marine woke up the sleeping fire teams. The word was sent to the foxhole next to Damon's. Shocked, in disbelief to see an enemy getting so close, they slipped their M16 fire selectors into fully automatic mode. Simultaneously, at least six Marines opened up. The clear and present danger was eliminated as dozens of rounds penetrated the enemy's body. He had most likely died before his body hit the ground. Now all they could do was wait until morning.

No team was allowed to go out and search the body because there could still be others waiting in ambush, and it was important to not give away their exact position any more than they had already. Waiting often became the hardest part. Perhaps the discipline Pfc Damon had learned in boot camp—things like patience, not jumping every time a fly landed on him or a mosquito bit into his flesh—was paying off. Yes, patience and waiting, had now become virtues.

## Heart Shot Five

*It all started when the word came down. From the first mention of it, more adrenaline got pumped into the Marines' bodies. It was a funny thing, this adrenaline surge. Who knew, at such a young age that adrenaline affected the body with more than just a flight or fight response? Damon sure hadn't figured it all out, but it was there. Marines never run, so the adrenaline, of course, was there to fight. Yet, the adrenaline never went away, even after the clash was over.*

*Damon prepared himself, unknowingly, for the raging of the adrenaline rush that seemed to stack one layer of adrenaline upon another. First contact, another layer. First kill, another layer. With each encounter, a man is thankful he is still alive. Unknown to them, however, was that the building up of chemicals, produced by their own body, could have effects well into the future. That was, if they got out of 'Nam alive!*

*Was Pfc Damon afraid in Vietnam? Funny question. The combat encounters came so quickly that his training kicked in, he did his job, and thought about it later. This had become Pfc Damon's world—kill or be killed—and survival moved into first place. His thoughts flashed back to before the Corps. Damon had lived in an entirely different world then. Would he be a different person after his tour of duty, or would he even be around? The only people who died faster than the Marines were the Viet Cong or NVA who were foolish enough to engage them! Damon's longing for home and thoughts of his new bride gave him encouragement to stay sharp, learn, listen, and live on to fight another day.*

# Chapter Six

## *Point Man on Patrol*

EARLY IN THE morning, Hotel Co. received orders to move out. Pfc. Damon was on point that day, closely monitored by Fire Team Leader Gerioso and the all-seeing eye of their squad leader, Wild Wit. All seemed well as the squad moved into the open rice paddy, dried after its seasonal harvest. In the distant tree line was a village of straw houses within a peculiar setting of banana trees and bamboo stalks. All was quiet.

An explosion shattered the silence. Out of nowhere, AK-47s and machine guns rained a hail of bullets all around the Marines. The main assault seemed to be exploding from the tree line ahead of them, in front of the village!

Not a good position for the Marines to be in. Caught out in the open, the only place to go was straight ahead, into the waiting enemy's barrage of gunfire! A small rice paddy dike lay ahead, about twelve inches tall. It was the only cover from the ruthless hail of bullets and mortars.

The Marines inched their way ahead and buried themselves behind the small berm, each of them trying to become one with the dike. Returning fire was all they could do to help suppress the bullets driving into the ground around them. Welcome to the no-win scenario that Marines usually avoided. How could they get out of this one?

Fortunately, Hotel Company had a forward observer with them that day. It was a lieutenant who was qualified to call in air strikes on an enemy if Hotel Company was pinned down. As the fighting continued, the forward air observer called in two F-4 Phantom jets from Da Nang Air Base. In what seemed like minutes, angels from heaven appeared. The silver-streaked Phantoms made a pass to confirm the enemy, then approached again, fast and low.

The first jet released high explosive bombs well behind Hotel Company's lines. At first it looked like the pilots had released too soon. How in the world were these bombs going to not land on the Marines? A sense of panic set in that caused Pfc Damon to push himself as deep into the rice paddy as possible. The bombs sailed effortlessly past the Marines and landed perfectly on target, in the tree line in front of the village. It sounded like the earth itself had been blown in two as huge amounts of rock and soil were ripped from the ground. But the most beautiful sight ever seen was yet to behold. The second jet came in at another angle and released shining capsules that turned end over end before striking the ground. Damon had heard of these shiny bombs, turning end over end to mix their contents and to better provide the fireball payload known as the napalm bomb.

Damon could not resist poking his head above the paddy dike just to get a look. A fireball erupted before his very eyes as the exploding napalm jelly splattered everywhere. It burned with such heat that even at 150 yards away, he could feel the intensity of it burn his forehead like an instant sunburn. Damon reasoned that the enemy ambush site must have been a whole lot hotter because, with the napalm, the enemy then had nowhere to run or hide. The enemy firing had ceased. There was no more movement from anyone at or near the village.

The order came down for them to search the village, which meant any structure was to be thoroughly checked out, and the grass roofs were to also be searched. Within minutes, a loud explosion was heard deep within the village. A new order quickly came down to cease and desist searching. This seemed a little odd to Damon, especially when the next order was to burn all standing buildings to the ground.

Damon protested to his fire team leader Gerioso about burning people's houses.

LCpl Gerioso yelled to Damon, "Follow your orders, Lane. You'll see why soon enough!"

They lit grass huts first, starting with the walls. The flames quickly spread up the dry grass to the roofs, which were closely woven grass. Once all buildings were burning, the Marines quickly exited the village.

Still wondering what was up, Pfc. Lane helped a few villagers, who had been hiding, to escape safely with the Marines. Within seconds, the flames engulfed the houses and every house exploded with such intensity that once more the ground shook. Every Marine was glad that someone had discovered a booby-trapped house early and the trap was set off without injury.

It all began to make sense to Pfc Damon now. Perhaps the "salty" Marines, those who had been there before, had experience he needed to not only listen to, but learn from. This village had become a sanctuary for Viet Cong troops, and the houses used to store and hide weapons and ammunition. As reality again began to nag Damon, he realized just what this small country had become! It had turned into a country that served two masters, the Americans by day, the Communist by night.

For the rest of the operation, Damon walked a little humbler and vowed to keep his eyes peeled just a little sharper, and learn all he could from the salty Marines who knew all too well the cost of war. They found many enemy bunkers, which had to be searched then blown in place. Sometimes, if the bunker was larger or had large stashes of ammunition, engineers traveling with the Marines would prepare charges and blow the bunker and its contents to smithereens.

Another hard thing for Damon was blowing up rice caches, which provided food for people who lived in the area. But this operation was done in a free-fire zone, which meant anyone living in this area was considered enemy or Viet Cong sympathizers. The food supply had to go. During this operation, Hotel Company literally destroyed the enemy's ability to resupply ammunition and booby traps, and the food to fight on another day.

Hotel Company continued to be probed that night by enemy sappers. However, alert Marines were able to detect them and ward them off with volleys of M16 fire and hand grenades. The next morning, on patrol, Pfc Lane found an enemy hat that appeared to have a round shot right through the bill, separating the hat from its rightful owner. Small patches of blood splattered the inside, which pretty much meant that was the man who had tried to kill Marines the previous night. No body, just a hat! This happened quite often in night skirmishes. The enemy had a habit of dragging off their killed and wounded, perhaps to discourage Marines from reporting enemy deaths. Damon was sure bodies were hidden in small tunnels or caves until the Marines moved on.

Pfc Lane hung on to the hat, his first war souvenir. Would keeping the hat bring him good luck, or would it be the karma that would send him to an early grave? Damon weighed the thoughts and tucked the cap deep into his backpack, willing to accept the odds.

Toward the end of Operation Lynn River, Hotel Company was hit really hard. As reality set in one more time, Damon wrote home to his family requesting, of all things, more rifle cleaning gear!

## Heart Shot Six

*A strange malady seemed to be developing within Pfc Damon Lee Lane. Going from a culture of preservation back home to one of destruction of property in 'Nam ate at Damon's ability to reconcile the events. Events like building houses in America, and blowing them up in Nam! Questions began to arise. Were these people really human beings just like the Americans? The Viet Cong's use of innocent women and children to promote their savagery just didn't seem right. Burning houses—or hooches, as they were called—didn't seem right, either. Yet, the villagers had provided supplies and storage to warriors who were more than willing to blow Marines apart at a moment's notice.*

*Damon didn't really feel too bad about what had been done once he understood all the facts, yet homes were gone, people were dead, and life went on. Why hadn't he felt bad? Was he becoming a hardened Marine, without feelings, or was there something else going on? During battle, he experienced an adrenaline rush, which seemed to only add to the rush he had gotten the last time the bullets flew. And after hearing what the enemy NVA and Viet Cong had done to the Marines at the Khe Sanh Firebase just the previous year. Damon knew he was on the right side.*

*Overall, Damon felt secure. He felt justified. He was serving his country with the greatest fighting men ever known, the United States Marines! The thought, though, still haunted him. The thought that they had the power to literally destroy ones home, belongings and their lives. This never set lightly with most Marines. He had friends who were there one day, then the next day they weren't. He thought about this and prayed that he would not be the next one that "got it!"*

# Chapter Seven

## *Medical Evacuation*

IT WAS SIMPLY called medevac. The term was slang for medical evacuation—for the unfortunate ones who were killed, wounded, or had any other good reason to get to the rear area. Most of the time, men were sent out with the next chopper, unless it was a medical emergency, which usually was the case.

Operation Lynn River was winding down, and it had been pretty much like the operation before this one. Orders were to search and destroy all enemy strongholds, which included ammunition, bunkers, and any persons caught carrying any type of weapon. The Marines encountered two regiments of NVA, a force that was 1,200 to 1,700 hundred strong. The Marines knew from intelligence that Go Noi Island, which they were working their way into, had always been a hot spot for enemy activity. This area consisted of sand, much like the ocean beaches back home, yet was infiltrated by ten-foot-high elephant grass, which could slice open a man's arm if he simply brushed up against it. Many a Marine sliced open his ear or forehead as he tried to chop his way through the razor-sharp grass with his trusted machete.

The name Lynn River didn't quite seem right because Damon wasn't sure he wanted to use such a calm name to pursue these gooks into an area where visibility was lacking and the enemy could ambush them around every bend. Nevertheless, orders were given, the enemy was pursued, and into the tall elephant grass they went.

Damon could sense the uneasiness in the lay of the land. It seemed that the enemy was watching their every move. This made him wonder who was really in charge of the area. As he penetrated the winding trail between the grass and piles of windblown sand, he noticed the smell coming from the island. The place smelled more like a sewage plant than the jungle paradise that it should have been.

Deep into the trail, a few sniper shots rang out. Damon hit the dirt in a reaction that he would repeat all too many times over the next few months. As a matter of fact, Damon wasn't on point at this time. His rifle was slung over his shoulder, the barrel capped with aluminum foil to keep the drizzle from getting inside.

Much to his surprise, as he was hitting the dirt, he emptied his weapon in the direction of the sniper, and it was empty before he hit the ground. This quick reaction was mandatory if you wanted to survive in this place. Off to the right of the trail, a land mine had been discovered and unearthed; perhaps the engineers would blow it in place later. As the day wore on, the most pressing matter was the heat of the day, causing sweat-drenched bodies and aching backs from humping 80- to 100-pound packs all day. Humping was the word the Marines used for packing and carrying every-thing they needed in a solitary pack. It felt heavy, and it dug into their shoulders, causing an aching from the straps being impacted deep into the shoulder muscles.

Sometimes, forward movement was one step at a time. Only when the firing started was the aching in the back forgotten about. The adrenalin took over and the heavy weight became secondary. This pattern was repeated day after day, hour after hour until the cover of darkness set in and the Marines dug in one more time and welcomed the solitude of the night.

Deeper into Go Noi Island, the Marines dreaded the night. The sand dunes made it impossible to dig regular foxholes, so the Marines set up a perim-eter the best they could. As the evening cooled down and the darkness settled in, Damon noticed his body temperature didn't seem to decrease and he just didn't feel right. He called the corpsman over, who took a look at Damon and checked his temperature.

Damon's vital signs must have been off, along with a very high temperature, because the corpsman gave strict instructions on what would be happening next. He was given medication along with orders to get as much sleep as possible. He was to sleep only, no fire watch or ambushes that night. The corpsman also took Damon's rifle away from him because Marines had to be in their right minds to have a loaded weapon. As uncomfortable as Damon was without his rifle, he welcomed a full night's sleep. A common malady with these symptoms was malaria, which could cause bouts of mental instability. The corpsman confided in Damon that hallucinations were common and they didn't want him to shoot up an enemy that wasn't there. By any means, a night off was good for Damon, and the remnants of Hotel Company kept a safe watch out for the encroaching enemy.

Throughout the night, Damon struggled with high temperature, chills, and delirium. The corpsman wanted to medevac Damon, but it was just too dangerous unless it was an absolute emergency. Perhaps the next day a chopper would be able to get in and get him to the hospital.

The next morning Hotel Company had to move out, along with the other companies. The enemy was on the run, and the Marines needed to track them down. By now, five other Marines had been wounded along with Damon who of course was just sick. The wounded Marines were left in an open rice paddy as Hotel Company pursued the retreating enemy. The wounded were assured there was a chopper on its way. The medicine Damon had taken had helped a little, and his rifle was returned to him since he was the most able-bodied person awaiting the chopper. His job was to help control the bleeding if it started again, and keep an eye out for any enemy who might like to take advantage of the situation, but he was mainly kept occupied by waiting and looking for the helicopter. The heat of the day only added to the misery of the wounded Marines as they lay there, wounded and dirty. By now, the stench of blood had become repulsive. It was well into the afternoon before the helicopter arrived. Nevertheless, it was good to be on board and heading toward the battalion aid station somewhere behind their lines.

The chopper landed and the Marines huddled together in a circle, waiting for triage. Damon made sure the Marine who had been shot through the back of the neck, straight through and out the front, was the first to go in. Believe it or not, this Marine could still walk and pretty much had all his faculties! Damon helped him get up and into the waiting stretcher to be taken into surgery. The corpsman couldn't understand why Damon wasn't going first because of the blood and his obviously deteriorated mental state. Damon insisted that the corpsman get the wounded in first because he was only sick and it wasn't his blood on his stained and filthy jungle utilities.

After the wounded were taken into surgery, Damon was led into a separate tent-type room for evaluation. By this time, the sun was setting, and there seemed to be a premature darkness settling in. Damon reasoned that whatever bug he had was causing his system to struggle once again to maintain balance between life and death. His fever spiked suddenly, and the corpsman frantically tried to get IVs into Damon's arms, but it was useless. The veins were collapsing, partly from dehydration and partly because of the stress of the day. Damon was not an expert on anything except staying alive, but he suspected the rigors of combat were stressing his now-sickened body beyond measure.

He underwent a quick evaluation by the medical team, then they used a sponge alcohol wipe down to help cool him, and a new helicopter was called in to rush Damon to the hospital in Da Nang. It seemed like only a few minutes until Damon heard the helicopter's blades whooshing the air outside. As he was escorted inside and seating securely in the helicopter, Damon noticed it was fully nighttime and the darkness that made Vietnam a scary place had now engulfed everything.

The engines began their usual increase in noise and vibration as the chopper lifted off the ground. Suddenly, the whining slowed, and the big green beast of a chopper settled back on the ground. *Oh God, what now?* Damon thought. The rear of the chopper opened by its hydraulic controlled hatches. As the lower half of the tailgate settled back down on the tarmac, four Marines ran forward with two body bags in tow. The bodies were swung into the back of the chopper at Damon's feet. A sense of dread overwhelmed the already weekend Marine.

This really wasn't the way Damon wanted to travel to the Naval Air Station Hospital in Da Nang. The trip seemed to take forever, and Damon thought about the men in the bags. Were they anyone he knew? Were their families advised yet? A new sadness swept over him as he just sat there and stared. His heart went out to them, and he resisted the urge to unzip the body bags and see who they were.

Once inside the hospital, Damon was again given a thorough examination, hot shower, and proper treatment, which included more tests to determine what exactly was going on. Treatment worked slowly, and Damon soon felt himself slowly responding to the medication, clean environment, and a bed with actual sheets. That night, the excitement once again sprang into action. Not the exploding of rockets or mortars, but crunching and gagging inside his mouth! A nurse had made his rounds and put a thermometer inside Damon's mouth as he was sleeping. Due to the remnants of chills and shakes, Damon had bitten completely through the thermometer, exploding glass and red iodine inside his mouth, causing the gagging reflex. Once awake, Damon was able to pick out the glass shards, which could have caused unrepairable damage, and spit out most of the iodine. Perhaps the iodine had some type of healing effect because Damon improved steadily and rapidly over the next few days.

Soon, Damon was able to get around much better and was able to venture outside for fresh air. There, he met another Marine who was on his way home. He had been in the hospital for a while, but his time was up, and he was being released to go back to the world. Damon talked with him for quite a while and only remembered two things about him. One was his name was Larry and the second was that Larry told him before he left, "Take time to know the Lord." This seemed like a strange comment, since Damon had gone to church most of his childhood. Nevertheless, Damon tucked the comment away, much like he did a lot of other things that were said or happened in Vietnam.

Once Larry was gone, Damon walked around the outside of the hospital. The tin roof overhangs provided shade over the cement sidewalks that surrounded each unit. There were some Vietnamese children playing, and Damon stopped to chat with them. One boy about the age of ten was with the children and had a white handkerchief over the opening of his mouth. Damon asked him what was wrong, and the boy lowered the handkerchief and exposed the problem. His lower jaw was gone and Damon could see straight down into his throat. There had been no repair possible, and the handkerchief was there to keep out flying insects and to keep other people from having to view this grievous wound. Other than that, the Vietnamese children were laughing and having a good time, which cheered up Damon immensely. Even the young boy was in superb spirits and acted as if nothing had ever happened to him. Damon felt so much older than the children, but it actually seemed like it had been only a short time since he was their age.

The day came all too soon for discharge and return to combat. Damon was to rejoin his same unit and find out the results of the rest of the operation. Upon inquiring during the exit interview, Damon learned his diagnosis had been changed from malaria to streptococcal pharyngitis. This was good because malaria required treatment for the rest of your life, and Damon was already sick and tired of being sick! As he boarded the awaiting helicopter, Damon felt like a new man. He was anxious to see his old friends again and be brought up to speed on current events. Or, maybe not!

## Heart Shot Seven

*During his stay in the Hospital, Damon was challenged on several fronts. One was the idea that war was producing many casualties. His heart told him that this was part of keeping the world free. It was also the idea that foreign powers should not be allowed to persecute their own people. But, what did he know about all of this? Yet, he saw the damage war was doing. To the land, the people and especially the children. The thought that a young man would have to live with having no real mouth seemed to bother Damon, more that it bothered the boy!*

*As Damon thought more on these things, the words from Boot Camp, the training and all the hardness of the experience began to make absolute sense. This was why they wanted the Marines to be tough. So they could take it, and keep going. It all made sense!*

# Chapter Eight

## *Ambushed*

WHILE DAMON HAD been recovering in the hospital, 1st Squad 1st Platoon was sent out on patrol to investigate the whereabouts of the enemy who had so easily hit and run the company a few days before. As the squad got farther and farther from their lines, Sgt Letty was walking behind the point man, Pvt Meloy. Sgt Letty had the squad leader, Wild Wit, behind him, and the rest of the squad was strategically placed in fighting positions as they moved along. As they penetrated enemy territory, Sgt Letty looked to his left and observed some tall elephant grass, on his right was more tall grass!

Several hundred yards ahead was a bamboo tree line and Sgt Letty all of a sudden got a *feeling* they were about to be ambushed. He quietly reached over to Pvt Meloy, put his hand over his mouth, and pulled him to the ground.

Meloy looked at him and said, "You almost gave me a heart attack!"

Letty put his finger to his mouth. "Shhhh. Let's crawl back to the tree line behind us."

When they got back to the tree line, they set up a defensive perimeter and discussed what they should do next. Squad leader Wild Wit thought they should go around that area, bypassing and avoiding the ambush. Sgt

Letty's idea was to hit the enemy head-on. However, if this was the typical three-sided ambush, they would be nothing but dead meat before the day was out.

Wild Wit questioned Sgt Letty about what he had seen. Letty said, "Nothing, I saw nothing. But something tells me they have machine guns on the left and right in that tall grass. And ahead in the tree line are NVA riflemen waiting for us to walk into their ambush!"

Gerioso, the fire team leader, who voted to go around said, "Okay, do what you want, but whoever decides should walk point." They went with Letty's plan

Perfect ambushes meant a lot of guys would get killed. Wit said, "Here was how it was going to happen!"

Sgt Letty would walk point, with Meloy behind him. Wild Wit would walk third, with his radioman, Crae, walking fourth, and Dizzy walking tail-end Charlie to make sure no Viet Cong could sneak up from behind them. Then they made their way up the trail as if they were walking into the trap. WOP would take a fire team on the right flank into the tall grass and take out the machine gun nest. The new guy, Olsen, would take a few men to the left and take out the other machine gun nest.

It was a genius plan. Just before Wit, Letty, and their team got into the kill zone, they jumped into a huge bomb crater—one they knew was just ahead and to the right—for protection. Within seconds, the enemy machine gun nest opened up ahead in the tree line. The radioman lay in the bomb crater, talking to HQ, and Wit stood straight up in the crater so he could see the enemy ahead. Sgt Letty and Meloy fired burst after burst of M16 rounds at the tree line ahead, with their rifles set on fully automatic fire, to put as many rounds downrange as possible! There seemed only seconds between loading magazines into their rifles and ejecting the empties.

As Wit continued to watch for the enemy to assault them, he looked down at the radioman. Wit yelled, "What the hell are you doing down there? Get up here and fire back!" Now the radioman had gotten HQ on the line and Sgt Frenchie, Hotel Company's Sergeant, worked with Wit to help get air support to the battlefield. Somehow, Frenchie was able to get Wit patched straight into the pilot of the F-4 Phantom.

Wit kept busy that day, keeping an eye on the enemy in case they planned a frontal assault. He kept an eye on his men in the bomb crater who were returning fire toward the front. His radioman needed more than a little direction on engaging the enemy, and he had to make sure Dizzy, watching their rear, didn't fall asleep. He had been known to do that. Then there were the teams out on the left and on the right. If this hadn't been enough to do, he also needed to keep an eye out for the Phantom that was soon to arrive. Damon often wondered what being a squad leader would be like. Now he knew.

The fire support plane was supposed to be there by now, and Wit said over the radio, "Where the hell are you guys?"

The pilot said, "Look straight up," and as Wit looked up, he saw the F-4 Phantom making its initial pass, right over their heads and straight for the enemy target ahead!

After the initial pass, the pilot radioed Wit. "Be advised, pull your men back. There is a second tree line behind the first tree line where they're shooting from! And the gooks in the second line are coming out by the hundreds!"

It had been an ambush alright, but more like a planned slaughter! By now the two fire teams had driven off the machine gun nest, who had turned tail and run when they realized they had been outsmarted. The Phantom delivered high explosive bombs on both enemy positions and then did the usual napalm run, which burnt everything it touched. After napalm had splattered around and turned to a firestorm of hot jelly and fire, the enemy fell silent. The quick thinking of Wit, Sgt Letty, and their men had once again saved the day.

Damon often wondered how Sgt. Letty knew. He'd seen nothing. Did he smell fish on their breath that they probably had for breakfast? It was partly his training, for sure, but Damon mostly believed Sgt Letty was hearing from a force that knew more about him than he knew about this force.

It was early February, and already two of Damon's "boot camp" buddies had been wounded. One buddy, called Ox, had stepped on a mine, which turned out to be a partial dud, but blew with enough force to break both of his legs and remove a few pounds of flesh from his butt! He recovered well, with no permanent damage other than scars for life that he would never see. The other Marine, called Roy Rogers, spotted an enemy bunker with a cache of weapons. He took an incendiary grenade and attempted to throw it inside the bunker. An enemy soldier shot at Roy as he released the grenade, which exploded prematurely, causing severe burns on both of his hands, but the enemy, the weapons, and the hiding place were all destroyed.

Meanwhile, Damon's friend and boot camp buddy Bouncing Freddy caught two Viet Cong penetrating the area on the company's perimeter. Bouncing Freddy grabbed a grenade, pulled the pin, and threw it in the general direction of the approaching enemy. When the grenade exploded, his adrenaline was pumping him into overdrive as he swung his M16 into full automatic action and emptied two of his twenty-round magazines into the enemy. Freddy said, "I don't even remember changing the magazines when one had emptied!" After the shooting stopped, two Viet Cong lay dead and had entered the realm the Marines called "wasted."

These were the stories that brought Damon back up to speed about what had been happening. So much for good news! Yet, Hotel Company was being resupplied with food and ammunition. It seemed they were getting more ammunition than when they were supplied the first time. Damon again inquired about where they were going and why so much ammo.

The reply was, "We're going into a hot zone, and most likely will need all that we can carry."

Damon knew what this meant, so he didn't need to know more. Wherever it was they were going, there would be plenty of enemy to go around, so he let it rest. Once again, he put his life and confidence in the brave men who led his squad, platoon, and company, and pondered the events about to unfold.

After a few days' rest, Hotel Company was inserted into an ongoing operation. The final supplies came in by truck hours before the command came down to move out. Even though this area of insertion was not considered a high enemy area, the insertion would begin from our present position moving rapidly inland. It would be another mixture of rice paddies and bamboo stands that allowed plenty of cover for Charlie, another name given to the Viet Cong. The area awaiting us was half secured, half enemy hideouts and did not give them any relief from enemy snipers.

The paymaster had been flown in to deliver the monthly pay to the troops. They only had to come out once a month and were responsible for the cash as well as the funds the troops wanted to send home. It always seemed kind of odd for an officer to be sitting at a little collapsible desk and chair out in no man's land. As Pfc Damon reported for fund disbursement, a shot rang out from a distant tree line. Everyone hit the deck. Some sniper tried to get off a lucky shot but, as usual, their aim was off. However, as Damon was working his way back to his fox hole, he noticed the corpsman and men from another company frantically bandaging up a downed Marine!

Apparently, this sniper had not missed, and Pvt Gardner had been shot in the stomach. There was a look of terror on the Marine's face, and his breathing became heavy and labored. They tried hard to save him, but it was easy to see the blood was squirting out of the pressure bandages, and as Gardner's face turned ashen gray, they knew he was gone.

Sometimes, it's best to look the other way, Damon reasoned. He had not wanted to get too used to seeing bloodshed and death. Of course, Damon knew tomorrow there would be payback dealt on the village near where the sniper had shot from. This was the law of the land. Nobody messed with Marines and got away with it. Not for long. As Damon did a final retreat to his foxhole, he muttered to himself, "I've seen enough of this," He quietly sunk down inside the newly dug foxhole.

Less than two months in-country and Pfc Damon had been baptized into combat, seen Marines wounded, watched others die, and been medevacked himself. The realization that this was going to be the longest thirteen months of his life was setting like freshly poured concrete. With the reality of battle and the certainty of death, Damon thought of his newly acquired bride Christina, his parents, and a home that seemed so far, far away.

# *Heart Shot Eight*

*It had seemed like months from the time Damon was medivacked from the present operation of search and destroy. But it had only been a few weeks. The carnage that Damon observed around him was unbelievable when thinking in the mind set of back home. But this was a different world. It didn't seem like life was that important. And in the heart of a nineteen year old teenager, it didn't make sense, after all a thought from his past kept floating into his mind: "We hold these truths to be self evident, that all men are created equal." Were these people created the same as us? What about the sniper that shot a Marine in the back, confining him to a wheelchair for the rest of his life? And what about the one that shot Gardner?*

*As the days rolled on and Damon tried to connect the dots of what was happening, it seemed the puzzle would not be solved. He settled in to do his job, the best he could and not only survive this war, but bring as many home with him as he could. As it had been said before, you mess with Marines, somebody will pay. That was soon to unfold as the Marines prepared for an operation called Eager Pursuit.*

# Chapter Nine

## *Close Encounters of Da Nang Defense*

ONE OF THE main duties of all the 26th Marine Battalions was to protect Da Nang in a continual operation called Da Nang Defense. Marines rotated in and out of firebases among the hills overlooking the enemy routes of infiltration into Da Nang. Such was a place called Hill 10. An artillery battery was stationed there, but they needed protection around its borders. Grunts—infantry Marines—filled these positions nicely. These rotations took place between major operations and when their naval fleet was temporarily dispersed to another area.

Hotel Company was trucked to Hill 10 and as they worked their way up the winding road and around the cliffs, a 4x4 truck lost control and plunged down the steep embankment. The driver's head was caught and crushed under the truck. He died instantly, but all the Marines in the open back of the truck were able to get out alive. It was a sad day for such a disaster to happen. Marines also guarded the tanks at Hill 10 by forming perimeters made of foxholes and berms.

One of the tank encampments was very near Damon's foxhole, and they had gotten sighted in by firing their fifty-caliber spotting gun. But after getting set in, they moved the tank a little forward, which made the "big gun" lurch down a little lower than they had planned. Damon was on watch that night, and the tank got a fire mission. *Boom!* The big gun fired with no warning, and it seemed to be right above Damon's head! Damon was so surprised that he grabbed his M16, twisted around, and almost fired on the tank! That would have been bad news for Damon, but by this time the reactions to being fired on had to happen quickly. Fortunately, for all involved, Damon realized what had happened and all was well—except for the ringing in his ears and perhaps a little hearing loss in his right ear.

If that wasn't enough, the moon came out that night and just as Damon was recovering from the tank incident, he noticed a long and devilish centipede come out of the berm in front of the foxhole. It ran completely around the foxhole's perimeter and right at Damon! It looked like he was heading straight for him and was hell-bent on getting his poisonous jaws on into Damon's leg. After a quick retreat, Damon returned with an entrenching tool and made short work of this communist centipede aggressor.

After a few days there, they pulled out and were sent to another firebase that needed outside day patrols and night ambushes. This firebase also had another outpost up on the hill, overlooking the firebase, which required at least one fire team to guard it each night.

When it came to 1st Squad's turn to do a night ambush, they prepared and slipped out, under cover of darkness, down to a rice paddy beside a road into a compound the Vietnamese ARVNs (Army of the Republic of Vietnam) controlled. The ambush was to surprise any unauthorized night activity and also to protect the ARVNs from enemy assault. The night was uneventful and as the darkness gave way to hints of gray and the warmth of the sun began to peek through, First Squad began to break camp and get their gear together.

As they were doing that, an ARVN patrol left the compound on a day patrol. When they saw 1st Squad beside the road, they opened up on them with automatic rifle fire and the bullets whizzed between the twelve guys of the squad. The Marines all hit the dirt just as the idiot ARVNs realized their mistake.

Damon was amazed that not one bullet had hit anybody, not one! The incident also proved that Marines do have patience and don't always have a finger on the trigger, ready to blast away at anything that moved. Lucky for the ARVNs that day that the Marines had that patience, because once a Marine starts shooting, they usually finish the task!

Hotel Company was moved from this compound after a few weeks to camp by another road that came by another village near the outskirts of Da Nang. Word had it that the Viet Cong and NVA were in the area. Intelligence reported that a quarter-mile south of where they had set in was a creek. A couple hundred yards north on the creek was a footbridge that the enemy was using to get into a better position for a Da Nang assault.

As soon as darkness set in and the blackness of the night made visibility zero, 1st Squad sneaked out of the perimeter, traveling south on the road until they crossed the creek. They then turned north to follow the creek. They were keeping a sharp eye out for the footbridge that was supposed to be hidden in the darkness. They were only about halfway there when Damon spotted something moving in the blackness on the other side of the creek. He stopped the squad and motioned for Wild Wit to come up and take a look.

Wit looked but thought it was nothing. "You're seeing things, Lane," he whispered.

"No, no," Lane said, "I don't think so. Just watch what looks like dark trees." As he looked one more time, the "trees" began to move in the same direction First Squad was going. Perhaps intelligence was right that the enemy was using the bridge. The Marines were going to mess that up.

Wit had already canvased the area with his map long before he came out on patrol that night. He told the squad that there was a large draining ditch just about twenty yards away from their position. He then ordered them to work their way into the ditch because they were caught out in the open where they were.

As they worked their way toward the ditch, one of the Marines canteens began to clang as they speedily ran for the ditch. The unknown force across the creek immediately opened up on them, spraying bullets in every direction. Exploding mounds of dirt and the cracking of rounds coming in everywhere told them there hadn't been a moment to spare. They all knew that Lane had saved their asses that night.

Damon was told later that he pulled one man into the ditch just as bullets whizzed by them. Damon didn't remember clearly, but thought a Marine had gotten in his way, so he'd just knocked him into the ditch to save himself! Regardless, he was very proud of the fact, though, that he had spotted the other column before they had spotted them.

Wit ordered a green signaling flare to be shot into the air, which would indicate we were friendly American forces. As the pop-up flare was shot, it burst red, and the shooting started again.

Finally, in frustration, Wit just yelled out, "Who are you guys?" They turned out to be a Combined Action Platoon (CAP) Unit with Vietnamese and American Forces. Wit went over to talk to them and found out they were going to do an ambush on the other side of the bridge across from where Wit's was going to be. When Wit returned, he told the squad, "We're going back to the compound. We don't need two ambushes close to the same place!"

Wit radioed in and let the company know the squad was coming back in ten minutes, and he would pop a green flare so they wouldn't get fired on again. As they neared the lines, a green pop-up was shot off. To everyone's surprise, this pop-up was red too, the color of enemy forces. It turned out that the whole box of flares had been miss-marked or some crazy mistake had been made.

The next day, Damon found all the food had been stolen out of his pack except for a ham his mother had sent from home. A few of the village boys who hung around the compound heard about Damon's dilemma, went home and had their mother fix Damon some food. When he asked what the meat was, they said, "Duck." He figured it was dog meat, but tasted good, and he was grateful for it! In Vietnamese, the sounds of dog and duck seemed a lot alike.

So Damon's Vietnam saga continued, and one thing could not be figured out. Why were friendly forces running into each other during night ambushes? Why were the ARVNs so trigger happy? How could two ambushes be planned on the same night right next to each other? These questions could never be answered from the end the grunts were on. This problem arose from somewhere else. These weren't the only times night patrols and ambushes ran into each other at night. Some of the time, it was an accident. But usually, as would be found out later, someone was not watching during the planning phase. Or perhaps the planners had no clue on what really went on out in the bush.

Other things always happened, even in temporary duty stations like at Hill 55. This was pretty much skate duty for Hotel Company because they just had to coordinate their patrols and monitor their bunkers at night. One day, another company of grunts were in the next valley over and had run into several Viet Cong. As the Marines "lit them up"—slang for shooting the daylights out of them—they tried to run away and ran right into Hill 55's valley.

Damon happened to be walking across the compound and saw three or four Viet Cong run into the grass that was growing in the rice paddy about three hundred yards away. The Marine gunners quickly loaded a 55-mm flechette round and fired. Within seconds, all the Viet Cong were down, and that was the end of them. A flechette round is an artillery round that bursts in the air and sends out little shards of metal like darts or nails and shreds the target. It was a perfect shot, perfect timing. Soon the other valley, where the operation was wrapping up, had been stabilized. *Just once in a while,* Damon thought, *things come together and everybody gets on the same page.*

As Hotel Company was leaving Hill 55, the new group of Marines were already moving into the area. Much to Damon's surprise, in the lead Jeep was an old friend from boot camp. His name was Mike Churn. Damon had always liked Mike, and it was good to spend some time talking with him. It was the last time Damon would ever talk to Mike. A few years later, Mike would commit suicide, an event that would happen to veterans 22 times a day in America. It would become a national tragedy!

## *Heart Shot Nine*

*Damon began to realize that even in the most secure places in a war-torn country, one can get killed, maimed, or injured. One of the things that helped Marines to survive was that they had learned to adapt to any given situation. Of course, when one stepped on a booby trap, there was no time to adapt. The explosion would rip through the air and whatever was around it! No time to adapt. No time to jump away or run. If there were time between the tripping of the device and the actual explosion, perhaps there could be some escape. But the booby traps were fierce, quick, and once set into action, few escaped! Booby traps perhaps worried Damon the most. They were well-hidden, and the surprise detonation would give no time to think.*

*One Jeep driver, who was 6' 4" tall, went on a pleasure drive one morning down to the neighboring village. On his return, he ran over an enemy mine. The blast was so huge and intense that they only found about 4' of his body. Damon realized, once again, there were no safe places in Vietnam. No place of protection for their hearts!*

# Chapter Ten

## *Operation Eager Pursuit*

THE FINAL TROOPS were staged, supplies finalized, and the truth of Operation Eager Pursuit was revealed. As if they hadn't had enough already, Hotel Company was ordered back into an area known as Dodge City. Really. A place called Dodge City, in Vietnam. It was also known to be in the Arizona Territory. Such strange names. Damon checked the map, and sure enough there it was. It was an area with the name, not a village or town. Damon wondered if the Dodge City name had a different meaning than an area. Perhaps it was an action that needed to be done? They had been there before, and the memory of it still lingered on in his mind. It was a real place; they were going back in, and the reason they were going was because Charlie had moved back in after they left the last time. No surprises there!

The enemy was there, alright. On the last operation, Damon had spotted a small opening in the jungle-infested ground just off the trail. To the other side of the trail was a dried rice paddy. But to the left was an opening, well-camouflaged and hidden, but nevertheless it was there. As Damon began to explore the crevasse in the jungle floor, the very petite opening appeared to enlarge itself the deeper into the earth it went. Damon carefully worked his way through the opening, checking each side of the narrow space for booby traps, snakes, and tripwires that could pull a grenade into your face seconds before it exploded.

Once inside, Damon stared in disbelief at what he had found. More than a bunker, this ten by twelve-foot room was an emergency aid station for wounded enemies. On the dirt walls were bamboo supported charts and medical diagrams that would alert a physician to where the most important organs were. Candles were scattered around to help light the room with just enough light to allow a procedure without alerting the Americans who were searching for them. There was a makeshift cot and a hammock hanging in one corner, no doubt used for recovery.

Fresh blood-stained bandages lay on the ground, no doubt dropped to the ground as the aid was given. No time for neatness as new injuries would have to be treated. The blood-stained bandages looked like they could not have been more than an hour or two old. After doing a more thorough check for weapons and other trap doors that could lead to other bunkers, finding none, Damon left the hospital bunker, leaving it intact. Of course, the usual protocol was to blow up all bunkers to deny the enemy a hiding place!

As Damon looked back at the dirty den of refuge, he made the personal decision to leave the bunker alone. This small doctor's office would stay open one more day to relieve the pain and suffering of an enemy that had already suffered, bled, and died as pawns in a political system that gave no choice to its participants. Right or wrong, Damon was at peace with his decision that day. It proved to him that he was still in touch with his humanity and that the forces of darkness had not totally invaded his heart. But, then again, they were about to go back in. Maybe he should have destroyed that hiding place.

The stage again was now set, and the sound of helicopters in the distance alerted them that supplies, more ammunition, and maybe last-minute mail would be inserted. To the horrible surprise of the Marines, the choppers only brought them more ammunition. No mail, no chow, just more stuff to hump back into Dodge City. Where was their ride? It had been two days since the men had a meal and they were sure there would be C-Rations that day, but none came. Just ammo!

Tempers flared which happens when blood sugar gets low, and a young Marine named LCpl Di had had enough. He grabbed his M16 and was going to shoot down the helicopter had it not been for Sgt Letty and a couple other Marines who wrestled him to the ground. It was amazing how many guys it took to hold the little Puerto Rican down.

Only a Marine low on chow, low on patience, but high on exhaustion could understand Marine Di's reasoning. Perhaps he had sent them a message. Just before dark, and none too soon, more choppers winged their way through the sky and delivered much-needed C-Rations to the Marines. A quick meal, and as darkness began to settle over the companies of Marines, the order came down, saddle up, they were moving that night under cover of darkness!

This area had not been a cakewalk either. On one patrol, as Pfc Damon was walking point, he spotted an NVA soldier lying to the right of the trail, up on a grassy knoll. Damon got down and called for Wild Wit to work his way forward, the squad leader confirming the sighting. Wit sent a fire team off to the right and forward to out-flank the hiding enemy and then surprise him with a side assault. As the fire team, led by Sgt Letty, approached the enemy, they could tell he seemed to be alone. Carefully working their way to him with weapons ready, he still lay in the same position.

Within a yard or two, the Marines realized this soldier was either asleep, wounded, or dead. Upon careful examination for booby traps, trip wires and whatever else the enemy might try to pull, they realized the soldier was dead, but there were no signs of wounds on the left side of his body. As they rolled him onto his left side, they noticed his right side had rifle shots every inch of his body, from his head to his foot. He must have been caught out in the open when the Puff the Magic Dragon AC-130 gunship worked the area over ahead them. These gunships could cover every square inch of a football field with rounds in just seconds. It proved once again to be a weapon feared by many enemy troops and a welcome companion to the Marines below.

Now that the darkness was complete, the battalion-sized unit began to move out. Hotel Company was selected for point platoon, 1st Squad was selected for point squad, and Pfc Damon and Sgt Letty would trade off walking point until the objective had been reached. And so it began, hump a while, trade off, rest then begin all over again. The cooler night air did not lower their body temperature much because of the energy required to pack all the supplies. The whispering and complaining the Marines were doing was because they were going back in "there," plus now it was in the dark. The main concern was that they hoped whoever had planned this one knew what they were doing!

The column continued to move as quietly as possible, yet the fear of Dodge City was on everyone's mind. As the column moved and worked its way through the jungle, it became mandatory for a rest every click or so. A click was a thousand yards and with the packs, heat, and uncertainty of what lay ahead, the rest times allowed the Marines to recoup, get their bearings, then pass the word to move out again.

Somewhere in the column, the order to move out did not get passed properly. So the front column disappeared into the night while the rest of the column sat waiting for the word. As time passed, the last Marine in the front column reported that they had lost the rest of the column. Once the mistake was discovered, mistake number two was made. A Marine was sent back down the trail to hook up with the stalled column. In the black of night, it was hard to stay on the right trail. The Marine got off the regular trail and onto another trail that put him out in front of the stalled column. Sensing enemy movement in front of them, another Marine raised his rifle and fired. The first round made a loud popping noise, then *ummmpff*. A second shot and a responding *ummmpff*! Unknown to the stalled part of the column, the enemy turned out to be a Marine.

An exchange of radio transmissions from the front of the column to the stalled column shed some light on the incident, and it was learned that a Marine had come back for the column. They worked out a way to connect the columns without any further bloodshed. This was considered an accidental shooting and the experience was chalked up to a lesson learned.

When the Marines reached the objective, which was a river by a blown-up train trestle, the Marines set up a perimeter the best they could. The wounded Marine, who turned out to be the company radioman, was wounded badly but it was thought he could make it if they got an emergency medevac in that night.

As Damon moved to a forward position next to the river to set up a night watch, he sent word back down the column that the forward fire team was setting in. Remembering a smooth spot a few yards back, He moved back to that position to drop his heavy gear. The smooth spot happened to be an intersecting trail that crossed the main trail they were on. However, due to the blackness of the night, the trail had not been discernible. It was by now the very early hours of the morning, yet the darkness remained thick and visibility was almost zero. Damon relaxed a little knowing Hotel Company had reached its objective and there would be no more humping that night. His shoulders ached, sweat was pouring down his back, and he was eager to relieve himself of his pack, ammo, and extra munitions for the mortar team.

At the smooth spot, Damon first lowered his rifle, which he'd carried in the ready position all night. He could already feel the coolness of the fresh air administer cooling to his back as the heavy pack was swung off his back and onto the smooth spot below. Of course, Marines had to bend forward and down at a funny angle to swing the heavy pack off their back, contorting their back as they went. Bending forward once more to relieve himself of the last of the supplies and to get a canteen of water that was on his duty belt, Damon got a little better look at the smooth spot. He recognized from experience that the smooth spot was a foot trail crossing over the one they had just come in on. This was not a good sign.

As Damon began to straighten up, *he* was there! The he was an enemy soldier, coming down the foot trail, oblivious that the Marines had sneaked back into the area under cover of darkness. Had this event happened a few minutes earlier, Damon would have taken him out with his M-16 rifle, but it now lay under the weight of his pack and gear. It might as well had been packed away in the armory in Da Nang. The only fighting material available to Damon at this point was his K-Bar, the Marine fighting knife, which was handy, and Damon's bare hands of course. Marines were trained to take out an enemy without weapons, but Damon went for the K-Bar.

Thoughts flashed through Damon's mind! *What if this guy is booby-trapped and tackling him blows us both up?* He shuddered at the thought of his shredded and powder burnt body being shipped home. These thoughts caused a very moment of hesitation, and as Damon reached out to engage and kill the soldier, the enemy sprang up and away like one of the jack in the box clowns. He must have jumped ten to twelve feet and disappeared along the bank of the river. By now, the rest of the fire team had seen what happened, and they tried hard not to laugh out loud by how horribly the enemy must have been scared. They joked later how he had to have messed his pants when he ran into the Marines!

Intelligence was made aware of the situation, and they figured the man was a messenger sending plans out to other enemy units in the area. Now they knew the Marines were there, and tomorrow would even have bigger surprises!

The next day several search and destroy patrols were sent out. Somewhere down the same trail that had led the enemy soldier to the Marines the previous night, an enemy travel bag had been dropped. Inside, the Marines found enemy maps, marching orders, and information that there was an NVA regiment in the area. This meant there were 1,200 to 1,400 hundred NVA hiding in close proximity. Among the other things the soldier dropped was a small wallet-like packet that had pictures of a young man, his wife, and two twin girls. They suspected that this belonged to the messenger and he now was the luckiest man in South Vietnam. Damon often wondered if the man had ever made it back home or was he just another statistic like so many other enemy soldiers? Damon secretly wished that this man had made it back to North Vietnam and lived happily ever after, with his family.

There was a ritual always preformed in Dodge City. At 2 a.m. sharp, the enemy would open up on the Marines that were stationed on top of the railroad dike. The train tracks had long been removed and the Marines had dug in the best they could. Every night, 2 a.m., you could set your watch by it. The sky lit up for at least a quarter-mile while the enemy engaged the-Marines with automatic rifle fire with tracer rounds. The Marines returned fire with volley after volley of M16 and machine gun fire. Within minutes, the advancing enemy was turned back and the night fell silent again. The most puzzling of these ordeals was that nothing could be found the next morning. No empty rifle casings, no dead bodies … nothing.

The NVA had become experts in the ability to drag away their dead and wounded. How they were able to police the brass they expended remained a mystery. The entrenched enemy had so planned these confrontations that they had spider holes, tunnels, and underground bunkers to drag their dead and wounded for hiding and safety. Their objective for this was to deny the Marines an accurate body count or bragging rights on how many had actually been eliminated. Their reasoning was based on their idea that the Marines' morale would be decreased if they saw no fruit from their labor of fighting.

Soon after the firefight, there was a whirling sound way above the Marines. They recognized it, but they could not see it. A helicopter had been called in for an emergency medevac. Due to the recent nighttime engagements with the enemy, a total blackout was called, and the chopper was guided down by a strobe light on the ground, which was a flash of light just for a second every few minutes. This gave the brave chopper pilot some direction because there were no other guiding lights. The Marines hoped and prayed that the pilot kept the blades of the chopper away from the railroad dike because their heads were not too far away.

Once the helicopter was on the ground, some red lights on the dashboard could be seen, but they were out of the enemies' sight. Within minutes, the wounded were handed over to the crew chief and the chopper lifted off. One of the advantages of the Vietnam War was the Marines could have their wounded in a hospital within twenty to thirty minutes instead of days. Damon often wished he could give a handshake and a big thank you to the Marine pilots who so bravely came in for their wounded.

The next day, the Marines sent out day patrols for most of the day. On returning to the railroad dike, it was 1st Squad's turn to be up on the dike, exposed to enemy fire. As the afternoon drug on, there was mail call that day and believe it or not a whole pallet of Campbell's soup was delivered to the troops. As the mail was handed out, Damon was surprised to get a letter from his dad. It was the first letter he had ever received from his dad, since his mother usually did the writing. Most of the Marines by this time had changed from their combat boots into tennis shoes and were going up and down the railroad dike, exchanging food, cigarettes, and letters from home.

Damon just sat by his pack, reading his letters when two salty Marines came walking up the dike. Once they reached Damon, a look of shock came over their faces. They said, "Don't move. There's a booby trap just behind you." Turned out there was a mortar round buried in the dike that had machine gun clips packed all around it. It was just waiting for someone to step on the little point of the round sticking out of the ground and *whammo*! Lights out for the one who stepped on it.

In disbelief, Damon looked at the booby trap and noticed many a Marine had walked by it that day. It was almost like an unknown force had put its hands around the booby trap and said, "Step anywhere but here, Marines." Upon closer inspection, there was not a footprint within 1 inch of the device, and the triangle-shaped untouched area looked too uniform to be an accident. When the reality of this situation set in, Damon had gone numb inside. That seemed to be what always had happened when he had experienced a close call. Perhaps this was a way of protecting his sanity. The engineers were called up, and it was decided to blow the trap in place as to avoid any possibility of further injuries. When the engineers blew the ordnance, the plume of black smoke, metal, and dust rose about 75 yards into the air. Damon didn't know if he was just lucky or if he owed a debt of gratitude to those two seasoned Marines? Or better yet, was there an unseen force at work that day?

## *Heart Shot Ten*

*Damon thought, with all their training from boot camp and infantry training, the Marines had learned not to mumble and complain. Yet they still grumbled about returning to this horrible place. The operation which included going back in under cover of darkness, overall, netted 420 dead, wounded, or detained NVA who thought the battalion had left and wasn't coming back! Well, the brass fooled the enemy that day, and once all the Marines were aware of the success, it all made sense and they all felt better about it.*

*In Damon's heart, the events once more raised the bar on the amount of adrenaline one should be used to. He recalled how just working his way at night through the jungle infested with enemy caused an increase in anxiety. His orders were not to measure the adrenaline, but to find the trail and find the river. The job was done. The firefights proved to be an awesome display of firepower. Few Marines died during this operation, but many of the enemy had.*

*As Damon tried to wrap his mind around his near-miss with the booby trap, he settled down once again. And once again, his thoughts turned to Christina ... and home.*

# Chapter Eleven

## *The Assault of Hai Van Pass*

THE MARINES WERE pulled out of Dodge City and the Liberty Bridge area. Good riddance to it. The area had seemed like Death Valley to them, because life did not seem to have much value there. Besides the feeling of death in the air, the area reeked with it! In fact, at the last firebase they had patrolled by, there were two dead bodies beside the road in the concertina wire. They were small, somewhat mummified, and they believed they were left there as a testament to the enemy. The message was loud and clear. If you want to probe their lines and sneak through their perimeter, that would be your fate. Nonetheless, it seemed eerie because they were still human, enemy or not and the discovery that these were the same two bodies that had been there on their last trip through chilled their bones.

Hotel Company moved along Highway 1 along the route to Hai Van Pass. This was bunker duty, which allowed them to get some much-needed rest. It was considered skate duty, which meant very little combat except for sapper charges once in a while and sniper fire. Hole number one was attacked on the third night with probing, rockets, and hand grenades. The enemy hit hard and fast, then disappeared into the night in the same way they had come in. It was unknown if any enemy were wounded or killed and Hotel Company only reported narrow misses.

Upon talking with them further, it was found out the Marines in hole one had hired a skivvy girl (prostitute) to spend the night with them, prostitution being an all too familiar tragedy of war and its effects. The Marines were pretty sure that she had set up the whole attack herself, although she could not be interrogated because the Marines were smart enough to not report her presence.

Soon after the incident, a message came down that Intelligence had learned that in the lull of combat over the last few weeks, the NVA were building up numbers in the very high mountains above the Hai Van Pass area.

All seemed quiet the next morning as the sun rose quickly into the sky. The sunlight felt warm and perhaps this would be another lazy day for the Marines on bunker duty. Early in the afternoon, the civilians were trucking their goods down the winding road to market in Da Nang. The trucks were lined up, working their way down the highway and around the treacherous curves of Highway 1. All seemed well and business was as usual for the many merchants excited to sell their wares in the nearby city.

Without warning, just up from bunker three, a horrific explosion challenged the restful day. *Boom*! An explosion slammed into a truck, heavily laden with rice and merchandise. *Boom*! Another explosion took out the passenger side of the cab. Viet Cong or NVA, in the confusion, scurried quickly down from the jungle, grabbed several 100-pound sacks of rice, and raced back up the mountain to their hideout. It had always been unclear how those scrawny little humans could carry such weight when it was doubtful that they weighed as much as the rice. Hit and run. That's what they were best at!

Casualties that day were one rice truck, several sacks of rice, and one innocent Vietnamese lady who had been literally cut in half by the explosion. In a short time, the truck was towed away, the casualties were taken away and the area was restored to normal. That was until the Phantom jet from the nearby airbase arrived and shot up everything within two hundred yards of the ambush site. After several passes and ordnance expenditure, the place returned once again to a peaceful area as if nothing happened. It was uncertain what impact the fire mission really had because of the thickness of the jungle, the steep terrain, and the uncertainty of where the enemy was hiding. What was certain, however, was the fact that the Marines were not going to let that attack slide. Hotel Company received orders to report to a staging area below Hai Van Pass to be helicoptered to the highest peak, well above the pass. It was an area where the sun didn't always shine, and it was covered in cloudy mist most of the time. Things lived there, things that usually didn't like humans, friend or foe.

Somehow a recon team had been inserted into the drop zone the day before. Their job was to blast away jungle, trees, shrubs, and anything else that would hinder the helicopters from making somewhat of a landing. Recon was the toughest branch in the Marine Corps. Most Marines didn't always know how they did their job, but they always got it done. These men, working in small teams, could be inserted anywhere, sometimes at great peril to themselves. More than once, 2$^{nd}$ Battalion did emergency extractions for their recon teams. It wasn't always a pretty sight!

As the morning light gave way to warmth and enough heat to dissipate some of the clouds high above the pass, Hotel Company began their insertion by helicopter to the mountain peak hardly visible from the staging area. The choppers labored hard to gain the necessary altitude, loaded with the battle-hardened Marines. Everything changes in Vietnam. Each altitude had its own issues, and the heat variances caused undue stress on the helicopters, depending on the temperature, humidity, and load. Of course, nothing changed the choppers' ability to function more than an enemy rocket attack or a few rounds shot through the glass window, taking out the pilot!

First Squad was in the lead chopper and headed directly into the landing zone. During the first insertion attempt, the chopper suddenly pulled up and veered to the left. A red smoke grenade had been dropped into the LZ and its plume was still spewing hot red smoke into the air. Simultaneously, both machine gunners opened up and the chopper began to circle around for another attempt. The crew chief came back and told the Marines to get ready. The LZ had more than likely been made by a gunship shooting the trees down instead of a recon team, and they were going to have to jump out the back as soon at the chopper slowed and got them six to ten feet off the ground. Without the recon team, the trees were still four to six feet tall, with trunks protruding upward. There was no place to actually set the chopper down. Jumping into this was no small task for Marines carrying 80 to 120 pounds of ammo and gear!

As the chopper quickly zoomed into the LZ and hoovered just for about thirty seconds, Wild Wit, Pvt Di, Manni, and Damon tumbled out the back, hoping to land on something soft. The thought of landing in a trap was always present. Behind them was the rest of the squad, led by Sgt Letty and a guy called Dizzy. The Marines were all wondering what had they gotten into! Twelve Marines in a hot LZ, alone until the next choppers could bring in the remainder of Hotel Company. Firing commenced not so much because they saw the enemy but because they knew they were there and wanted to let them know this was now their territory and they would hold their ground until the full force arrived. Within minutes of securing the LZ, which meant making a circle around the zone with Marines facing outward and watching for any signs of movement, the rest of the company arrived.

The mission was an impossible one from the start. They were to do search and destroy patrols on the jungle-infested mountainsides that were almost impossible to move in. The brass hadn't got this one right. The Marines tried their best to send patrols out, but there was limited success because of the terrain. Except for a few enemy bunkers they destroyed, very little was found of the enemy or their actual whereabouts. Funny thing, though, about being in a jungle at that altitude—funny, creepy things lived there! Weird things like centipedes that were poisonous and deadly, and snakes that hadn't been seen in other places. A haunting spirit of death and destruction seemed to hang in the air.

As the Marines descended the mountain trail, their first break came up, and they gladly sat down for a few minutes of rest. Pvt Di seemed a little preoccupied over something where he sat. This little Puerto Rican had found a large centipede, or it found him, and Di was playing with it with a little stick, preventing it from getting away. They could run as fast as any Marine, but it wasn't going to get away from Di. The centipede was ten to twelve inches long and its leg span had looked to be around four inches across. This had been the largest centipede anyone had seen in Vietnam.

The next thing that happened sent chills up and down Damon's spine. Di had sprayed the centipede with lighter fluid and set it on fire. The insect squirmed and contorted its body, rolling over backward to escape the impending flames. It did not escape, and the sight of it trying seemed like a devil in hell going through much pain and torment. It seemed to take several minutes but soon the charred body lay motionless and the Marines felt justified that at least one victory had been seen that day.

As the search and destroy mission started back up after a brief rest, the patrols did the best they could, but so far, the tally was two or three empty bunkers blown up, a few empty munition boxes, one dead centipede, and nothing more. One patrol came upon a bunker that had been so well hidden in the sheer mountainside enclosed in jungle vines and mossy type grasses that had the enemy been there, they could have taken out the whole patrol before the Marines even knew what was happening.

By this time, the searing heat of the jungle and the treacherous terrain were making it impossible to send patrols out laterally. One Marine had injured himself falling on the mountainside and coming to an abrupt halt on a rocky ledge. He was not able to walk, so a medevac was called in. The Marines could hear the helicopter high overhead, but all that they could see was a gurney being lowered down through the triple canopy of trees and vines. As the Marine was hoisted out high above their heads, they all noticed that the injured man had wet his pants. They weren't sure if it was from the injury during the fall or if it was from being extracted in a wire gurney that was now spinning and tipping forward and backward as it ascended into the waiting chopper.

Another stop for a break and the Marines made a head call. Head call was a term that meant going into the bush somewhere to relieve oneself. With shock and horror, most Marines reported there were worms in their stool, and they all thought they were going to die. The corpsman explained that at this altitude other weird things would happen, but they should all return to normal when a regular altitude was reached. Unconvinced, Damon thought about having the Puerto Rican fire the worms up with lighter fluid, but the call came down to move out. Move, now that was a word that usually made sense but not this time. Move could mean a slip or fall and even worse, a free-fall slide down the mountain.

Captain Winkman got very frustrated with this mission because of the impossible terrain. Once he realized they were in a no-win scenario, the captain called for his radioman to contact HQ. The conversation went something like this, "Bravo Six, this is Hotel Six, I am bringing Hotel Company straight down this gosh darned mountain. No more sweeps or patrols are being sent out! Every step is a danger, and I will not risk further injury to my men.! Hotel Six … out!" The conversation was over, and they were going home, or, at least, back to the base.

By now Hotel Co. was about half the way down the mountain. The trail veered a little to the left but had been destroyed by torrential rains that year. The only way down that part of the mountain was to rappel thirty to forty feet over an area of bald-faced rock. As each Marine took his turn on the ropes, some did it effortlessly and some really struggled. As Wild Wit proceeded down the sheer face of the cliff, the rope snapped with a twang, and he plummeted several yards to the jungle floor below. Half entangled in the rope and half-dazed from the abrupt landing, he remained stunned for several minutes. He refused to be medevacked because he wanted to stay with his men and somewhat dazed and in pain, limped along as the descent took them closer to home. With his back and leg injured, it was obvious that Wild Wit was anxious to be at the staging area where they could at least take a break from the God-forsaken mountain.

Everyone was dragging a little, not just the wounded, but they could spot the rice paddies and level ground in the valley just ahead. The falling, twisting, wrenching, and bruising coming down from the mountain had taken its toll on all sorts of body parts. Yet the Marines were willing to forget the trouble they had just gone through the previous three days as long as there was an end in sight. They were looking forward to some warm chow and a rack to sleep in for a few hours. At the lower altitude, the worms they'd acquired in the high jungle altitude were dying off. Good riddance to them.

As their bodies required a few days to adjust to the altitude and recover from body-wrenching torture they had just endured, they were allowed a couple of days to rest and recover. Since their staging area had been near the beach, those who wanted to could take a swim. Within no time, the Marines were their old selves again, and rumors spread that they might get some more skate duty in an actual compound again.

The next day, Hotel Company was transported up Highway 1 to a new outpost called Hill 358. It was a double-topped hill with two barbed wire encampments that had a very nice view of the mountain they had just traversed down. Special thanks were given to the Marine operations managers for this thoughtful act of kindness to Hotel Company. Actually, the men were just glad to be "inside the wire" for a change, even if the safety was only in their minds.

Once he had settled into the lower bunker, Damon recalled that as Hotel Company reached the rice paddies a few days ago, they knew they were almost to base camp. It seemed odd to them to walk on even ground and their gait seemed off. But they were ecstatic to be on level ground and to breathe the warm air with its thicker constitutions. Every Marine's mind went to the place of question. How in the name of God did any Viet Cong or NVA soldier ever survive in such terrain? Lesson learned ... none. But wait, there was more. At least the enemy knew that day that they could run and they could hide, but the Marines would come after them no matter where they struck from. They might not always find the enemy, but they will go anyway. But here they were again, looking up the side of the mountain, with a base camp on uneven ground.

Even working out of a base camp, funny things could happen. It was 1st Squads turn to go on a day patrol, down the hill and around the countryside, looking for any sign of the enemy. Pfc Damon was on point that day, and as he approached a creek, looking back to the column following him, he noticed the Marines were squatting down taking cover. Had he missed something? Preparing to work his way back up the trail to a hail of gunfire, Damon calculated his return and the best position to be in to outflank the enemy that was there. Wit had heard movement, and it was off to his left. Something was moving through the brush and grass and was sure to be upon them any minute! Chills ran down Damons spine as he patiently waited to get the first sight of the enemy. Yet, something seemed strange.

Wild Wit had called over another Marine to swap Wit's grenade launcher for the Marine's M16. After the swap, Wit rose from a squatting position and peered above the elephant grass. Bam, Bam, two shots rang out, and the squad began approaching the victim, lying dead in the grass. The biggest kill of the year turned out to be an elk that had wandered down another trail and into the waiting Marine squad, who were just waiting to kill something. This guy had a rack on him bigger than any they had seen for a while. The Puerto Rican, however, cut off the testicles of the elk and slipped them into his camouflaged jacket pocket and never mentioned them again. We were afraid to ask or think what he did with them. Wit said, "Leave the elk there. On the return trip, we'll take its head and antlers up on a pole and some juicy steaks for a barbeque that evening." That was exactly how it played out, and 1st Squad made many friends that night.

This small outpost, half secure, half a target for the enemy to abuse them, received many rocket attacks. Fortunately, the rockets were ill-aimed and did very little damage except to a few jungle plants. After a few times of this happening, the lieutenant got pissed off and ordered a 50-caliber machine gun to be brought up on the hill. This was perfectly alright with the Marines for two reasons. One was, it was added security because NVA and Viet Cong bodies did not hold up well when a 50-caliber round hit them. Second, all Marines got a chance to fan fire the new weapon, which was a whole new experience. Needless to say, that ended the enemy activity against the hills after that.

Second Squad drew the lot for the night ambush. They were supposed to sneak out through the wire in the above compound, sneak down the gorge below the lower compound, and set up about a quarter-mile below. As the night wore on, movement was heard below the lower compound, just below a rocky outcropping that overlooked the gorge. The Marines reported it to the command post at the higher elevation, and a sergeant came down and asked for a volunteer to sneak out with him to the rocky outcropping and observe while an illumination mortar round would light up the area once they were in place. Pfc Damon knew better, but he volunteered, and they squeezed through the wire and out to the outcropping. Once in place, they called for illumination, and a thump was heard at the upper compound. Within a few seconds, the sky lit up right over the gorge where there had been movement!

Damon and the sergeant had already locked and loaded and were waiting to release a barrage of fire if the enemy was trying to outflank them. Below, there was nothing, just grassy areas in the gorge but no one was there. The enemy must have figured out what was coming and took off. Or it was 2$^{nd}$ Squad trying to skate the ambush by not going out far enough. In the early hours the next morning, another patrol scaled down into the gorge, and sure enough there was plenty of signs that someone had been there. No big deal. Nobody died or got hurt that night, and nothing else was ever said about it.

First Squad was sent on a discovery patrol the next day, across the nearby creek and onto a woodcutters trail that led up into the jungle. As they neared the wooded area, they heard a loud whistling sound that sounded like a very large bird with lungs bigger than the elk they had shot a few days earlier. The sound was loud and penetrated the jungle to the point that earplugs would have been nice. Half whistle, half roar, Damon had never heard anything like that before. He looked back at the radioman, who had been in-country for some time. The radioman said, "That sounds like rock apes!"

No sooner were the words out of his mouth, when huge rocks were thrown out of the jungle trees. These crazy apes were hurling rocks and stones at the patrol. Being in an area that was not a free-fire zone, the radioman called for permission to fire. However, this was getting dangerous. The Marines opened up on the apes, which sent them scrambling to get away. As they went, they made weird calls to each other, and the trees bent and swayed as they hastend away. Of course, the call came back from the lieutenant to not fire. Right. Marines do not "not fire" under any circumstances when they are attacked. Best they could tell, the apes lived on to challenge yet another day anyone who dared to invade their territory!

As the Marines contemplated what just happened, the worst thing for them was that the lieutenant had denied them permission to fire. Another act of cowardice. And this wasn't the first time. Many Marines had been previously put in peril by the decisions this leader had made. The Marines just looked at each other, smiled and shook their heads, realizing the chicken lieutenant they had at the time was just a coward. In boot camp, the Marines were trained and drilled that Pvt Light Tap and Pvt Defense usually died. These two names were given to those who were not tough and would not engage an enemy. In war, Marines were to strike hard and fast, not soft or from a defensive position of uncertainty. This lieutenant was the worst leader Hotel Company had, because he had ordered both and it would cost the lives of more than one of them before their tour of duty was over.

## Heart Shot Eleven

*Damon realized that very few things could spike the adrenaline like going into a hot LZ. It did things to the heart. Yet somebody had to do it! These buddies of his— these brave, brave Marines—followed their orders to the max. Whatever the order, whatever the cost, they went! They took care of each other.*

*Yet they were unaware of the effects of sustained adrenaline on the body, soul, and spirit. At an average age of nineteen, who would have thought of these things? Surely not them. They were too busy staying alive and keeping as many of their buddies alive as they could. Yet, slowly and methodically, with each new ambush, each new firefight, each new sudden explosion ending the life of their friend, it seemed stress was piling up and being stored away ... but where? These were things Damon often thought about. And home seemed so far, far away.*

# Chapter Twelve

## *Transfer to Headquarters*

JUST ONCE IN a while, a Marine gets lucky. Squad leader Wild Wit had been called to the higher knoll of Hill 358. Within a short time, Damon was called there also. Wit said, "Lane, get your gear packed you're going to battalion headquarters. You're going because you know how to type and you have combat experience. Also, you're the only Marine in the squad who's married and the 'guys' decided you should be the one to go."

"What the heck?" Damon didn't want to be an office pinky, a guy who sat in an office while the war raged on miles away.

"You got no choice, Lane," Wit said. "It's already decided, and your replacement's already here!"

"Yeah, La-La-Lane," the little Mexican, Manni, stuttered. "You married, Marine, and you should go!"

Damon was just a little pissed off for even thinking of leaving his guys who this far had borne the battle on so many occasions. The order came down, though, and Damon Lane began packing up his gear for the hike out to Highway 1 in the morning.

As Wit returned to the lower bunker, he introduced Damon's replacement as John Michaels. LCpl John Michaels, if that made any difference. He was about Damon's height, a little stockier, very pale since he was new to

Vietnam, and he seemed kind of a quiet sort. Wit said, "OK guys, we got an ambush tonight. Damon, you're going out on ambush tonight, but you can walk tail-end Charlie, and you get to sleep all night unless we get hit."

Damon began to like this transfer a little better all the time! Wit reinforced the idea that Damon needed to go because if they got hit, he needed all the support possible from veterans, meaning those who had actual experience. The thought crossed Damon's mind that he might actually get a full night's sleep for the second time in Vietnam.

As the eerie darkness began to set in, the ambush worked its way out of the compound and into the nearby rolling hill, just out of sight and reach of the upper compound. If the NVA or Viet Cong came out that night to attack the hill, the Marine ambush would be there to short-circuit their plan. They would cut them off by outflanking them and reducing their numbers rather quickly. First Squad watched closely all night. Damon Lane slept! No action, no sudden call to arms. As the darkness yielded to the first light of day, Damon was jolted awake by the sound of absolutely nothing! He had slept all night. Could this have all been true? Was he really going to be transferred to battalion? By now, Damon realized that although battalion was his second choice, a sadness began to set in for his men who were still going to be in the heat of battle. And Damon, well, he was going to be in a safer place.

The final act before the squad's ambush would return to the base camp, was to police any gear they had laid out the night before preparing for a night fight with the enemy. The very last thing was to roll up the poncho liner that was used for a cover to sleep on during the night. It also helped to keep some of the mosquitoes from chewing their face and uncovered skin to shreds. Mosquitos, when they got near your ear, made a loud-pitched buzz just before they landed on you and dug in. These particular mosquitoes had to be enemy mosquitoes. They just had to be!

Damon was carefully rolling up his poncho liner to be placed on the top of his pack for the journey back to camp. Still in the kneeling position, he glanced up and made eye contact with his replacement LCpl Michaels. Michaels was white as a ghost, mainly from not being in-country long enough to get a tan or having had time enough to become a salty Marine like the rest of them. Or perhaps he was scared spitless from his first night on an ambush where the enemy was all around. As Damon's eyes met his, he recognized a look on Michaels' face! It was one of dread, uncertainty, fear, and lots of other emotions that could not be expressed. It was a look that exclaimed without noise but yelling nonetheless, *I'm not going to make it out of this place.*

Michaels had no way of knowing that day that he would soon be heading into an operation known to 1st Squad as Chu Lai II. Chu Lai was a hell hole of Viet Cong booby traps and just plain old hate for the Americans. Damon considered the look Michaels gave him that day. Marines can sense things and know things well in advance, especially point men; Damon had been one for several months in Vietnam and trained by the best, those who had walked before him. And Damon knew in his heart Michaels' fate was probably set. Chu Lai II might claim another victim, and the thought would haunt Damon for the rest of his life, as short as that might be. Damon never mentioned "the look" to anyone, yet it had been there. Even if he had, what difference would it have made?

Damon hiked out of the trail to Highway 1 an hour or two after coming back from the ambush. Not much was said as he left. A waiting Jeep escorted him quickly into Da Nang and battalion headquarters. Damon was interviewed by a major in charge of S-3 for final approval. Damon passed the interview and was introduced to a sergeant and a staff sergeant with whom he would be working closely.

S-3, as it turned out, was part of Headquarters Company's operation and planning division. They charted the ambushes and patrols and kept track of where all the Marines were day and night. This was a far cry from actually being out in the bush and engaging the enemy. Now, instead of being shot at and hearing bullets and rockets whizzing by during a fight, the action was heard over the radio as they kept close contact with all units night and day. Damon got a little more excited for the troops on the ground and cheered them on whenever the time was appropriate. The command bunker was a safe place, yet Damon kept his eye on the door because these pesky little Vietnamese were known to hit a bunker with satchel charges, killing Marines and officers inside.

As the days drug on, Damon often thought of his guys in 1st Squad. How were they doing? Were they all left? Yet attention to detail kept him busy on the job at hand. There were many corrections that needed to be done each day as new lieutenants would try to change their ambushes at the last minute, not knowing they were changing to an area where there was already an ambush. Before, they might have gotten away with such changes, but Damon had been there and had run into other units before. Not anymore! This was stopped, and many a boot lieutenant was very unhappy that a LCpl was denying them a change. Many of them soon found out, as the major made it clear to them, that a LCpl in this position had his authority, and it was like the major talking and not Damon. This policy saved lives because it kept the friendly fire casualties down to a minimum.

The other thing S-3 was responsible for was to send typed and mimeographed reports to regimental headquarters after they were reviewed by the major. This wasn't always the best because Damon didn't care much for the casualty list. And besides, it made him think about the two body bags that had been thrown into the chopper at his feet during Operation Lynn River.

Meanwhile, back at the 1st Squad, 1st Platoon of Hotel Company, rumors were being passed around that they were soon to be inserted into a familiar battlefield. The nightmares were coming true. They were planning another assault into Chu Lai. Tension mounted and stress skyrocketed as the Marines knew what was ahead. The plan was out, ammunition was delivered, and a sense of grief spread over the men. Hadn't they given enough? Hadn't they done enough? Hadn't they been to that place enough?

## Heart Shot Twelve

*Damon Lane knew why he was sent to the rear. He was married, he could type, and he had combat experience. He also felt a little disjointed that he had no say in the matter. Why him? For the first time, he began to feel a little hope that perhaps he might be one of the lucky ones and actually survive Vietnam. Yet he would miss the men who were his brothers. They were a brotherhood, where men became close, not in a crazy type way but in a way where they had each others' backs. Nobody could take that away. Damon felt some relief from the stress, but grief pulsated within his chest as he thought about those that he'd left behind. The Marines in the bush were the real Marines. It was those men who made a difference.*

*Damon would learn that in headquarters, he still would see the battle up close and personal. Experiences of war had long-lasting effects, and most of the time the ugliness was seen long after the battle ended. Such was the experience of the Battle of Chu Lai II. Even in the rear with the gear, Damon would soon come to the reality of the look given him by his replacement, Michaels.*

# Chapter Thirteen

## *Chu Lai II*

ALL THROUGH THE night, the sounds of helicopters coming and going made a deafening and haunting sound as the Marines below tried to get some sleep. The flight deck was being hounded by mysterious activity, much to the dismay of the men lying in their canvas racks, the name for their beds aboard the ship. They did not know what all the activity was about, but something was definitely going on. All they could do at this point was rest and prepare themselves for what was ahead. But as much as they tried, all they could really do was wait. They were used to waiting; it was part of their training from day one in boot camp. They also had developed the Marine slogan, "First to go. Last to know." Their job wasn't to know, but to go. And go they did and loaded for bear with food, ammunition, and an attitude that it was payback time for Chu Lai I!

The cards had already been dealt the previous night. A major offensive was planned to thin out the aggression of the communist forces threatening Chu Lai and Da Nang to the north. The Marines were inserted into the hellhole of Chu Lai. A perimeter was established, and more Marines were moved in until the Marines were satisfied they had enough strength to accomplish the mission. The other card that was dealt was that LCpl Michaels was now the new point man, taking Lane's place. On edge for some reason, Michaels settled in with the squad, yet he was haunted by something he just couldn't put his finger on. He had heard about Chu Lai, and he didn't want to be there any more than anyone else did.

As the day wore on and nightfall began to set in, part of 1st Squad was sent out on a listening post to spy out any movement or enemy activity. During the full moon and light-covered night, the boot lieutenant stood up and looked around, completely giving away their position. Fortunately, Sgt Letty pulled him to the ground and radioed in that their position had been compromised and they were coming back into the lines. They had to crawl back to their own lines while Wild Whit, the squad leader, notified the foxholes that friendlies were returning and to not fire. As the communication was passed properly, 1st Squad was able to slip inside the perimeter to a place of safety that was very much welcomed. It had happened none too soon, though. A squad or two of NVA had been seen moving toward the base camp, which caused a rapid exchange of fire between Hotel Company's 2nd Platoon and the NVA.

Wild Wits time in country was over. He was sent home. A legend had passed. Two tours of duty, not much more than a scratch or two. Unheard of for most Marines with combat experience for this long of time. No Purple Heart, no Medal of Honor. Only the pride within that he had done his job. One day he was there, then gone the next. He would learn once again that Semper Fidelis with Marines would last a life time. He boarded the plane called a "Freedom Bird" and disappeared from Vietnam. But never out of the heart of Damon and the men who so bravely fought and died together.

Because of the heavy concentration of enemy, listening posts were sent out every night. Viet Cong were spotted almost every night. Some were very close, some were farther out, but they were always working toward a common objective: kill Americans. Listening posts always carried the danger of being discovered, then being wiped out by the advancing enemy.

One listening post was watching carefully where hedgerows were surrounding flat areas of ground. The hedgerows only had a one-foot area between the rows that allowed passage to the next flat area. Meloy suddenly woke up Sgt Letty and said, "There was a gook who just walked by us and he had almost stepped on my face."

The night gave way to a full moon, and it was a little brighter than usual, yet dark shadows were cast from the hedgerows, making it hard to make out shadows. As the enemy came out of the shadows, he turned sideways to pass between the hedgerows. Sgt Letty raised his rifle and fired. Lights out, and one less enemy was left to deal with.

Not too long after that, Meloy handed the radio to Sgt Letty and said, "You're not going to believe this." Second Platoon also had a listening post just over the next ridge and the Marines on the listening post had spotted a Viet Cong and requested permission to take him out.

The Marine reported over the radio, saying, "The Viet Cong is carrying a mine and is digging a hole to place it in for a booby trap."

Of course, the Lieutenant's reply was, "Don't fire. You might hit the mine."

Wait, were they in a combat area or not? No matter which way the squad thought about the order that day, it hadn't made sense. What would the payment be for such cowardice as that of a leader afraid to engage the enemy? The biggest mistake was making a combat zone a non-free-fire zone, where every action had to be approved. What would be the cost of this misguided rule imposed on men who only wanted to help South Vietnam and reduce the number of American casualties? It would cost plenty.

At daylight, the listening post from 1st Squad were back inside the perimeter and settled back in for a few minutes of needed rest and sleep. Each foxhole had kept at least one Marine awake at all times during the night. A few firefights had erupted overnight, but the moon went behind the clouds, and all parties settled down for a few hours of rest. The listening post Marines were able to kick back and decompress from the intensity of the events that had required them to come so close to an ever-present enemy.

It was important to search and destroy by using patrols during the day and ambushes at night. First squad was selected to patrol with another squad as a wingman-type patrol. LCpl Michaels was on point that day and worked his way carefully through hedges, rice paddies, and small clumps of bamboo shoots. They were on edge that day because of the activity the previous night and knowing that somewhere out there, an enemy had been allowed to plant a booby trap. Sgt Letty was the new squad leader now and had been trained by Wild Wit. True to form, Letty cautioned all the men to be alert. When one gets the feeling that something just wasn't right, it usually wasn't. The trail narrowed just a little, which squeezed the men together into a smaller zone. This wasn't a surprise because the lay of the land was usually irregular, and nothing seemed out of place. But then, it happened.

There was no warning, no shining lights in the sky to give a glimpse of the future. There was just the loudest explosion, causing a ripping of ground from the earth. Dust and black smoke enveloped the squad in a quagmire of death. Visibility was nil, and the sound had deafened everyone's ears to what was happening. Yet body parts flew through the air and Marines lay wounded and bleeding on the ground. What had happened? It seemed like time stood still.

LCpl Michaels had sprung the booby trap. His body lay on the ground, totally black from the powder charge that had been set off. He was missing an arm and a leg, and his chest was ripped open. In disbelief, the Marines looked on, realizing that Michaels was still alive! His body was literally shredded yet he was hanging on for life. Four other Marines lay seriously wounded, but none like the point man, Michaels.

The body count that day was two Marines dead, four wounded, and a heavy anger set upon them as they realized this was the booby trap they'd been denied permission to take care of the previous night. The wounded would recover from their wounds and live on to fight another day, but they would never be the same. LCpl Michaels was still alive when he was medivacked along with the other wounded Marines to the air craft carrier, where medical personnel waited to patch their wounds and try to save the Marine. He was carried from the elevator outside the ship to the hanger deck and rushed up to the hospital.

LCpl Damon Lee Lane was on the hanger deck that day when Michaels was carried past. Damon saw him, but didn't recognize his charred body at the time. It was only later that the news came to S-3. Damon visited the other squad members who had been wounded and then was told that Michaels didn't make it. He had died that day. His last card was played. He lost the game.

So one more time this lieutenant had harmed the very men he was supposed to lead and take care of. LCpl Damon had no trouble believing that the lieutenant's actions had caused this because Damon had his own experiences with this officer, and more than once it had almost cost him his life. How many men would have to die because of ignorance or cowardice on their leaders' parts? Damon could not understand or justify in any terms the actions of this man.

Damon's heart went out when he saw some of his men in the hospital from being wounded in Chu Lai II. Four or five guys with bandages and coverings over their wounds from the mine that had been booby-trapped by an enemy who should have been dead already did not sit well with Damon. Sgt Letty had taken a huge piece of shrapnel in his upper sternum, cutting deep into his neck. As Damon stood in front of him and compared the level of injury to himself if he had been where the sergeant was; the shrapnel would have hit him between the eyes. Damon had always liked Sgt Letty even though he seemed to have a little deep-seated anger most of the time and appeared to not be in a good mood, ever. Nevertheless, the fault for this tragedy rested at the feet of the lieutenant and would not be forgotten any time soon.

Damon Lane had been at Battalion Headquarters for some time now. His sense of eminent danger had lessened since being reassigned to HQ. However, this day was considered a new adventure as he was flown from the aircraft carrier to the inland battalion command post at Chu Lai. Damon had filled very large paper bags the size of grocery bags with cookies the Navy cooks had made for the troops inland. Between the cookies and stuffing his combat pack with ice and sodas, Damon felt like he was going out on patrol again. This time his mission would be one of mercy and relief to the troops inland. Things didn't always pan out the way one would like, though, in Vietnam. The actual trip was to deliver a secret message in the form of a concealed letter to the major in charge of the battalion. Once the message was delivered, Damon distributed the sodas and cookies to everyone who would like some. They were consumed by the handfuls, and on the spot the men became indebted to the wonderful Navy cooks aboard the ship.

The company gunnery sergeant, Sgt Nault got the bright idea that they should take a sack of cookies up to an enclosed compound just off the beach, which was surrounded by concertina wire. As Damon worked his way through the sand up the hill, getting closer to the compound, he noticed there was a Marine looking out of the wire at him and talking on the radio. Within minutes, Damon heard his name being called from a small Black Marine who had run after him.

"Stop," he said, "You're walking in an unmarked minefield! Trace your steps back until your clear." Damon could hardly make out where any of his steps had been because the sand was dry, loose, and covered his previous steps well. Damon thought, *Well, I made it through once. Perhaps I'll make it through again.* He proceeded forward and arrived back at the command post with nothing more than a very angry attitude toward the gunny for not checking things out before sending anyone on any type of a mission—even a mission of mercy. In his mind, Damon could not figure out what the gunny had been thinking. He was, however, very grateful to the young Black Marine and also the Marine who had radioed over.

Damon was more than a little surprised, a month or so after the mine incident, when he and the gunny were working on a project. The gunny was older, appeared to be cranky, and more than once overly bossy. You would have thought Damon would have been used to being bossed around by then, but in one exchange, where the gunny pushed a little too hard, Damon exploded with words he had never planned to say. Anger oozed from Damon and he told the gunny where to go, what to do, and what for! The words were disrespectful, inappropriate, and unfair to a man just trying to do his job and do it well.

This caused the gunny to have Damon do a little physical training (PT) on the hanger deck while the gunny thought about what should be done. Damon actually got off easy because when he talked to the major about the incident, the major seemed to know Damon had been through a few things during his tour of duty. He said, "If you apologize to the gunny, this will be the end of it!"

Damon was more than happy to sincerely apologize because they were in a combat zone and the punishment could have been more severe than a mere apology. After the incident was over, Damon felt a small release in the tension brewing inside of him, yet he wondered what adrenaline, stress, or any other type of trauma could do to the heart of a man. Perhaps this had been a clue!

In the months that would follow, Damon would experience the effects of the adrenaline that had built up inside his body. He was hyper-alert most of the time. It seemed that any sound, especially unexpected ones, would make him jump and send him higher into alertness. Also, getting things absolutely right seemed to preoccupy his thoughts. He recounted many times when things were done wrong, and it only caused more calamity and injury, so it was necessary to be right. In his world, being right and keeping your act together allowed you to live on to fight another day. It had happened in the past and it was happening now.

Damon's mind flashed back to the lieutenant's habit of screwing things up, causing men to die. Damon had never considered himself to be an angry person. Yet his friends had died, and his squad had been severely wounded. Harsh resentment and anger seemed to be bottling up inside of him. All these injuries and death could have been avoided by an alert platoon com- mander, but indecision and cowardice had ruled the platoon, and it had cost them dearly. The creed of "an eye for an eye, and a tooth for a tooth" actually began to make sense to Damon. More than one boot lieutenant had met his fate on the battlefield—and it was not always from enemy fire! Some were wounded, some were killed, but the mode of punishment was usually a hand grenade.

This type of retribution was not actually acceptable to Damon, but neither were the actions that killed his friends. As a matter of fact, that type of action made about as much sense as the war! Yet LCpl Damon was not there to figure it all out. He knew he was there to stay alert, do his job, and help as many of his friends to come home as possible.

There were many platoon commanders who rotated in and out of Hotel Company. Most of them did an excellent job and were good leaders. However, the one they had then was not. These young Marines followed orders whenever possible, but the uncertainty of combat and the lack of good decision making caused their trust to be severely shaken. Trust was what Marines depended on. With trust broken, the men could easily allow hypersensitivity to injustice to set in. It would not be an easy tour now for this dysfunctional lieutenant, and because of him, confusion in combat situations and many calamities would unfold.

## *Heart Shot Thirteen*

*Damon began to realize that many things happen to a man who gets shot in the heart. Not so much from bullets, but when your friends, your squad, get hit and men go down, it affects you. But what would any nineteen-year-old boy know about these things? Very little. Yet they experienced them just the same! If Damon could have verbalized what he was feeling, it would have sounded week and unstructured.*

*Damon was beginning to understand the motto "Semper Fi" the Marines would often say. Always Faithful. But in his heart, there was an agonizing feeling that something just wasn't right. But who could know, at his age? And who would tell him? Nobody would, but as the reports from home were coming of protests against the troops, a new resentment was added to the jar, which was now a mix of stress, anger, and resentment.*

*Damon thought deeply about this. How dare any American protest what these brave men were doing? How dare they? The actual division of America that was hand-made and promoted by a certain part of society intent on rebellion was growing every day.*

*These things were unknown to most of the men doing the fighting, as well as the knowledge that we had landed men on the moon for the first time and that there was a rock and roll event that took place called Woodstock. That was okay, though, because wood stock, to the Marines, was the butt of an M14 rifle. It was the only wood stock they would know.*

# Chapter Fourteen

## R&R – Hawaii-Bound

SECOND BATTALION 26$^{TH}$ Marines had suffered many casualties. The brass decided to pull them out of Vietnam and send them to Okinawa, Japan, along with a fleet of ships for reinforcements. The battle-weary Marines also had time for a little rest, as well as receiving specialty training in Okinawa. After the stay in Okinawa, they would make a stop in the Philippines for jungle training, resupply, and a little more rest and relaxation.

Damon was picked to go with an advanced party to the Philippines, along with the major and a captain, to lay out plans for the troops coming by ship. It was rainy and cold when they boarded the C-130 aircraft in Okinawa, and it only got colder as the plane ascended to its cruising altitude. He tried to rest and sleep, but the C-130 was too cold, too loud, and the canvas seats were very uncomfortable.

As the plane landed at Clark Air Base in the Philippines, the tail end opened and the blast of hot air that engulfed the Marine party was unbelievable. Once off the plane, the major looked for the man with the lesser rank, which happened to be Damon. "Here Lane, carry my bag" he ordered.

This was of course in addition to Damon's own gear that he brought with him. The heat and weight made it very hard for this skinny young Marine to comply with this order. However, Damon remembered his out of order comments with the gunny a few months ago and did not say what was really on his mind. What he wanted to say was, "Sir, carry your own damned bag!" Sometimes respect had to be learned, and Damon finally had learned, if at least just a little. Keeping his mouth shut and following orders paid off. He was the only enlisted man on the forward team, and the major and the Captain provided good duty and took care of Damon during his time in the Philippines.

Unbeknown to Damon, the other Marines had been given an orientation about liberty before they got to the Philippines, but he didn't receive it because he was in the advanced party. One rule for going off base on liberty was that each different rank had to come off liberty at different times. Damon went into town and hung out with sergeants and staff sergeants, which meant he had to be in an hour earlier than they did. So when he returned to the base with the sergeants, he was immediately interrogated, yelled at by a Navy chief shore patrol, had his liberty pass and ID card confiscated, told he was in a world of s***, and put on a bus to be escorted back to his living area. Damon wondered if this chief had any idea what Damon had been through in 'Nam the last few months. And for a brief time, he actually thought of ways to take out this loudmouth person, but he let it slide.

Damon reported to the major the next morning to see if he was going to face a firing squad, sent immediately back to Vietnam, or what kind of punishment was due him. When the major asked what happened, Damon explained how he was not in the orientation because he was on duty with him and the captain.

The major just smiled. "You know, there was a sign as you left the base that explained the rules!" He handed Damon his ID card, smiled a little more, and said, "Just be careful next time!"

"Yes, Sir," Damon exclaimed loudly and did an about-face without saluting the major because Marines do not salute when uncovered and indoors. Damon left with the feeling he had gotten off easy because of working closely with the major. He was also learning that who you knew in this

Marines world was good for something. He was kind of glad he had carried the major's bag now and kept his mouth shut.

Not long after returning to Vietnam, a new plan was brewing. Damon had been writing his wife Christina and they were both planning to meet in Hawaii for R&R. He hadn't seen Christina since December, and he was missing her dearly. He had at least figured out one thing while being in Vietnam—Christina was the most important person in his life, and when this was all said and done, he wanted to spend the rest of his life with her.

He had been worried, though. When the gear was being unloaded in Da Nang, the S-3 safe holding his R&R money was swung off-ship by a cargo net. As the hoist moved to the Mike boat, the safe tipped and lurched into a funny position, and Damon panicked, thinking that it would fall into the bay. That might have been goodbye to R&R, if all his money had been lost. Fortunately, it made it safely to him, and in a few weeks, Damon was headed to Hawaii to meet the love of his life. It felt funny to not be in a war zone.

Damon's plane blew an oil pump on the way to Hawaii, and the pilot dumped hundreds of pounds of fuel into the ocean. They had to make an emergency stop at Guam. Several hours were wasted getting the plane repaired, and it seemed like 12 to 24 hours before they were able to take off again.

Once the plane was ready, a lone Marine was left lying by the building next to the plane. He'd gotten drunk and passed out. Damon thought the Marine should have been left because he'd gotten drunk, but two other Marines, who had more compassion than Damon, got back off and literally carried the man on board. Damon had just a little trouble understanding why he had not had any compassion for the Marine. Did he feel the drunk was holding up progress with his reunion with Christina? Yet, in his mind, he should have been one of the man's rescuers because he was relatively certain the man had only drank to ease his pain.

A few hours later, Damon was in Hawaii. After a quick orientation and a taxi ride to the agreed hotel, he was with Christina. It was hard to believe they were together again. They were not aware of the time. They just concentrated on their time together. Besides having a wonderful time together, they really enjoyed going to the International Market Place and taking a bus tour of Oahu.

One thing that seemed strange was when a teenage Hawaiian girl biking along the bus route gave them all the finger as she road along. It felt a little odd for that to happen. Damon later realized that she probably didn't like tourists, and besides that, she was a teenager. But Damon and Christina were in love, and it really didn't matter their outside circumstances so long as they were together—even being flipped off by a total stranger.

Of course, surfing came up since they were on Waikiki Beach. Christina had a cousin who was stationed at Fort DeRussy and joined them on the beach. Both veterans rented surfboards and began their saga. Of course, neither needed lessons. After all, they had reasoned that they "had this." After a few attempts, Damon was up on the board and rapidly heading inland. He hadn't accounted for the wave crashing over him from behind, sending him to the bottom of the ocean, and rolling him along the seafloor for what had seemed like an eternity. Finally, he got enough bearing to push himself off the ocean floor and to the clear blue surface above. Thoroughly exhausted, he had not been sure if he could even swim. Fortunately, another surfer had caught Damon's board, and once he surfaced, the man sent it flying toward Damon with a flick of his wrist. Damon was eternally grateful for this surfer who looked like he might have been a native Hawaiian.

Those few days in Hawaii would be remembered for eternity. At the end of their time together, they packed to go to the airport. Their departing times were close together, and Damon made sure Christina was all checked in and that she was in the right place. She said she felt better now that she knew where to be.

A thought came to Damon's mind, and he shared it with Christina. "You know, this will be our last goodbye. Next time we see each other, it will be for good." This seemed to really make them both feel better, and their parting just a little easier. Off they flew, in two different directions, both coveting the time they got to share with each other, and thanking God that their love for each other was still strong.

Four months to go now. President Nixon had ordered the Marines to shorten their tours of duty to twelve months instead of thirteen as originally planned. The Marines always had something to prove, and Damon felt the thirteen months was just to show the other branches how tough they were. Damon could have cared less about proving anything and was glad his tour was shortened. Even four months still seemed like a long time, but not as long as the thirteen-month tour had seemed back in January.

Damon thought about a lot of things during this time. He thought about the five Marine buddies of his that he knew had been killed. He thought about the many wounded and wondered how they were doing. He thought about his mom, dad, brothers, and sisters, but mostly he thought about his wife, Christina.

He also wondered if he had become a man yet. He had thought Vietnam could turn him into one since before he had been shy, introverted and very reserved. Yet, in combat, he had proven to himself that he could cut it. After that, it really didn't matter to him much what anyone else thought—with the exception of his men, his fellow Marines of 1st Squad, 1st Platoon. They mattered, their thoughts mattered, and he was very thankful to have met, served, and risked his life with these fine men, these very fine men. Words would never be enough to describe how he felt about them; there would never be words, and there would never be enough.

## *Heart Shot Fourteen*

*A short two-week stay in Okinawa, Japan, and Subic Bay, Philippines was a good respite. Even there, though, Damon could see the difference in how people lived, and it seemed strange that lives could be lived so differently. Coordinating training and hanging out with the brass had little appeal to Damon because his job was to do the job, not hobnob to be seen, gain rank, and move up the chain of command. His objective was to get home with all his body parts, his mind, and all his faculties in place. Perhaps this was not to be? Maybe this was what R&R*

*was for? To regroup and rethink and maybe get your head on straight. Who really knew? No one really knew. No one really knew what was brewing in the hearts and minds of our battlefield veterans, but many would soon find out!*

*R&R was a time for a warrior to unwind. A time, for a few days, where you were not an enemy. Anywhere but on the battlefield was kind of like R&R. Many men went different places on R&R. Some went to Australia, some went to Taiwan, and some just elsewhere. Some would sneak home for a few days, even though they were not supposed to go. But for Damon, there had only been one place for him to go and one woman for him to be with. It was Hawaii and Christina.*

*Sometimes when Damon was alone on bunker duty or downtime on the ship, he would think about Christina and what it would be like to be together again. Overlooking Da Nang Harbor while on bunker duty, he would imagine Sunday afternoon drives with Christina. It seemed foreign, but he could only imagine what it would be like cruising in the afternoon sun with his favorite gal. No one shooting at him, no booby traps, no cares in the world but one—his love for Christina. Oh, how time moved so slowly.*

*Damon also thought about other emotions while in Vietnam. Fear. Was that a real emotion? Even in battle, Damon didn't feel afraid. That seemed odd. Had some mysterious training helped him not be afraid? Or was the intensity of battle short-circuiting the feelings that should have been present? Shouldn't that number of bullets and other enemy fire that could surely shorten a man's life cause a sense of panic and fear?*

*For the most part, however, Damon had remained cool and in control when the bullets flew. Perhaps knowing his men had his back had helped with this? Or was it the training? Or was it that the adrenaline had topped out and he was now desensitized to the horrors of combat? What about his brothers in arms who had seen much more than him, especially Sgt Letty and Wild Wit?*

*A lot of questions bounced around in Damon's mind and heart, but they were never allowed to interfere with his main mission in Vietnam. A mission to help the South Vietnamese, help his fellow Marines, and get himself home safely. This was the peacemakers' job, this was Americans' reason to be in Vietnam.*

*Yet Damon heard that at home, people who knew nothing of war, nothing about communism, and nothing about respect, became violent and nasty in their attempt to interfere with the peace process. This shamed Damon, and it shamed America because these people, who knew nothing about war and cared nothing about freedom, had somehow become experts on policy. In reality, they had become pawns in the hands of communist propaganda and served the enemy instead of their beloved country, America*

*These were the thoughts and heart shots that Damon received throughout most of his tour in Vietnam.*

# Chapter Fifteen

## *The Long-Awaited Day*

A FEW MORE months slipped by, and Damon was glad that time had not stood still for anything. It never had and it never would. Sometimes that works against you, but now it was working for him. A few more days and he would be on his way home. The reports were coming in that there would be delays in getting out of Vietnam because of the number of men that qualified to leave. This had only made Damon a little more nervous because he was already a few days past his day to leave, but he was grateful to finally see an end in sight. He wondered what it would be like to have that long torturous year finally come to an end. It had been a year of uncertainty, a year of death and destruction, and a year that would live on forever. A funny sadness settled over Damon as he contemplated leaving his friends behind. Yet the overwhelming sense of home was wooing him, drawing him away to a new life, back home with his wife Christina.

Damon, now twenty years old, still had unsettling thoughts. Thoughts like, would he be the same person who had left a year ago? Would everything be the same when he got home? The worst thought was that he was going to have to get a job. Would anyone hire him for any type of job? Would there be a band at home playing the "Star-Spangled Banner" and welcoming him home? No amount of questions, even the hard ones, was going to

keep him from going home, home to Mom and Dad, his wife Christina …
and … a job!

There was a final inspection at base camp, receiving of orders, and a truck-
load of Marines waiting as patiently as possible for transportation to Da
Nang Air Base. Finally, they were all loaded into the 4x4 truck and were on
their way. The last apprehension and hesitation that Damon experienced
was when he was told to turn his M16 into the armory. His fighting days
were over, and he would not need it anymore.

"What?" Damon protested. "I'm not out of country yet and besides, I hear
there are protestors at home just waiting to raise havoc and they might
need to protect themselves." In Damon's mind it would be absolutely
appropriate to waste any long-haired, dope-smoking protestors if they
engaged him in any way. Waste, of course, meant they could be fired upon
and justifiably killed. Such thoughts should have revealed to Damon that
he was about to reenter another world, and his world would change again.

Finally, they arrived at Freedom Hill, which was the processing place to
get a final boarding pass and onto a commercial airline to fly to Hawaii,
then Marine Corps Air Station El Toro, CA. As Damon checked around
with some of the other armed forces leaving Vietnam, it quickly became
obvious why the system was backed up. All the office pinkies were getting
out early. Some were leaving a month before their actual date to leave. One
more time, Damon shook his head in disbelief that not only did the office
pinkies get all the promotions, but they got the early outs as well. They had
to do a lot of butt-kissing to get what they wanted, but Damon had always
hated that practice and therefore got a late exit from the country.

When Damon had arrived in Vietnam the previous year and seen some of
the younger women, he didn't really think they were attractive and pretty
much ignored even looking at them. However, when he was waiting for the
plane, an older mama-san was walking down by the gate, and he caught
himself looking at her like she was really something. Amazing what a year
will do to a man.

It was overcast that day, and nothing could be seen over fifty feet above the
runway. The plane was not in yet, and the men were getting antsy waiting.

Damon tried to keep his cool, but being without his M16 was making him more nervous by the minute. Was the plane coming? Was it going to cancel? Would he be mortared or rocketed upon its arrival?

Soon there was a roar somewhere in the cloud cover above. As Damon watched, a set of black tires and wheels poked through the clouds, then the most beautiful sight Damon had ever seen in his life. The commercial airliner was shiny and new. The Freedom Bird, it was called. Replacements quickly got off the plane, and a few minutes were taken to clean and re-board the plane. Damon finally reached his seat and wished they would hurry up. An eternity later, a South Vietnamese officer and his family boarded the plane, and it was all Damon could do to not yell out, "Let's get out of here!" He probably would have, but he feared they might throw him off the plane. So once more his training had kicked in about keeping one's mouth shut, a lesson Damon had already learned.

Soon the plane was moving into position for takeoff. Damon was breath-ing deep slow breaths. He noticed his shoes were digging into the floor of the plane, trying to scoot it along. The engines broke out into a very loud whine, and the plane began its final thrust forward to reach a speed that would allow takeoff. As the plane lifted off and Damon saw the ground getting farther away, he was mesmerized. So many things were going around in his head. Out of the right window, he spotted an F-4 Phantom that was escorting them away from the Vietnamese coastline. He saw an island below, and he sensed he was about to be out of harm's way. With one quick movement, the Phantom veered to its right and headed back to Da Nang Air Base.

Damon breathed a sigh of relief and wondered if the tension he had devel-oped over the last year in the pit of his stomach would go away also. It would not. No amount of relaxing, no amount of self-talk, and no amount of prayer (Damon wasn't really good at that anyway) could erase the tension in his stomach. It was like boots inside his stomach tied very tightly, like he had tied his boots before going out on patrol. Nevertheless, Damon was happy. He was on his way home. He was on his way back to Christina.

The Marines flew to Japan, first to clear out any gear they had in Okinawa and prepare for a flight Stateside. A short stop in Hawaii to refuel and get some type of processing done, and they were back on the plane and on their way. The civilians at the airport in Hawaii had funny looks on their faces as they just glared at the Marines. Perhaps even though the men were in clean uniforms, clean-shaven with haircuts, and were spic and span, the hardness of battle might have still shown on their faces.

The flight from Hawaii to California took about five hours. It was well into nighttime when an update came from the captain, who reported that they would be approaching the west coast in about a half an hour.

Just a few minutes nearer to the scheduled time, the captain came back on the intercom and reported, "Gentlemen, if you look out the right side of the plane you can see the lights of San Francisco!"

Damon was by the window, and when he looked, the bright lights over-whelmed him. To realize this was America and actually see the lights, those beautiful, beautiful lights. There could only be one thing more beautiful: his wife, Christina. Yet he had never, ever seen something so warm and welcoming in his life. The lights of San Francisco. He could not believe it. He was home at last!

Of course, Damon's melancholy brain kicked in. What kind of a welcome would there be? Surely the Marine Corps would have its band at the airport when they disembarked. Maybe the commandant of the Marine Corps would be there and present them all with the Medal of Honor? The anticipation was killing him, just like Christmas had when he was a kid and waiting for presents to be opened.

Upon leaving the plane, many men dropped down and kissed the ground. Damon did not. Instead, he kept his eye peeled for any protestors. He knew that if any attacked him or his men, he didn't need a weapon to take them out. The Marines had taught him very well how to end the life of another man with his bare hands, and he was more than willing to put an end to that nonsense of protesting.

However, the men were loaded on buses outside the airport and shipped to Camp Pendleton in the dark of night. Where was the band? Where were the medals for a job well done? They were met with silence that was more defining than any of the bombs that had been dropped just a few month ago.

The men were told to enter a barracks and instructed that they would be divided into groups the following morning and taken where they needed to be. Damon was shocked that first night. Old mattresses were rolled up on bunk bed cots. The men were instructed to select a cot and get some sleep. No blankets, no sheets, and no pillowcases.

Welcome home, Marines? Welcome home? This was a black mark on the United States Marine Corps! At this point, the welcoming committee didn't seem any better than the dirty filthy hippies protesting at universities around the country! Damon thought, *Shame on my Marine Corps! Someone should have been awake! These Marines just returned from war! Semper Fidelis had been gutted out and wallowed in the mud!*

The Marine Corps was not faithful to their troops on that day. It was a wound that ran deep and disrespected everything the Marine Corps stood for. Damon, being a very forgiving type of person, just shook his head and repeated the phrase to himself that he had been saying for a long time: "If I ever get out of here, they will never see me again."

The next morning, two groups were formed: those continuing in the United States Marine Corps and those who had come to the end of their enlisted time. Those continuing with the Corps were granted thirty days leave and left within minutes for home. The rest of them had to stay a few days and receive their discharge papers and be signed out. Of course, games were still being played by personnel who had nothing better to do than harass non-permanent personnel. This actually could have been dangerous for them to mess with these combat troops, and often it was only the sheer willpower of the combat troops that further altercations were diminished. There had always been enmity between combat troops and those that were called "lifers", men who made a career out of the military solely for the purpose of a career. The lifers went out of their way to treat all troops by lording over them with unreasonable demands. This sheer willpower came from the fact that any severe problem meant delays in processing and delays in getting home. So they put up with their crap. Not much had changed and not much respect for those who had borne the battle.

At last, the day arrived and there was a final signing out before heading to the airport. The captain gave his last personal speech to each Marine. When it came to Damon's turn, the Captain said, "Are you sure you want to get out, or do you want to reenlist?"

Damon responded, in no uncertain terms, "Sir, after I sign these papers, you are never going to see me again." With that, LCpl Damon and three other Marines hired a limousine taxi and rode first class to the Los Angeles Airport to begin their trip home. Within a few short hours, he was one his way home.

As he was walking down the airport concourse an elderly gray-haired lady ran up from behind him and said, "Welcome home, Lance Corporal." Damon didn't think too much of that at the time, but he learned to cherish her kind words over the next few years. Damon also remembered when he was heading to Vietnam at this same airport, he met an Army guy coming back from Korea. Damon, at that time, wished he had been coming home instead of going to some far-off distant land. Now, on his way home, he met another Army guy who was going to Korea. Funny how things work out. With that, Damon was on his way to his first and last stop before home, Portland International Airport in Oregon.

As the flight from Portland to Yakima, WA was a smaller flight, Damon had to change planes and had an hour or two layover. He was flying military standby, which meant there was a system used to prioritize standby personal. Damon, a veteran, was very high on the list and was one of the first called. However, there was a pregnant mother with a baby already in her arms and Damon could not let himself go before her. Damon allowed her to embark and waited patiently and secretly praying he would be next. He had made up his mind that other than this lady with the baby, he was a top priority. Damon was called, and onto the plane he went! Next stop, Yakima, WA.

Yakima was small town of around 50 thousand people, but at least it had an airport. It was home, a place of family, his roots, and most of all Christina. When he arrived in Yakima, it was cold. But it didn't matter to him. A small group of people were there to greet him, perhaps 12 to 20. There were people from his church, his old Sunday school teacher, her daughters, and his mom and dad, sisters and brothers. Then there was his friend Mick from Spokane, who had been his best man in him and Christina's wedding. Mick had lost both arms in Vietnam in a horrific explosion that nearly cost him his life. Damon wasn't really sure if he should reach out his hand for a handshake since Mick only had prosthesis or what? Instead, Damon just reached out and placed his hand onto Mick's shoulder and said, "Hi Mick." It seemed funny to Damon that he didn't really know how to greet his friend and had treated him differently when something major had changed in his life.

Mick had been at Nam O Bridge, north of Da Nang, guarding the bridge when he spotted bubbles in the water under the bridge. He prepared a small charge of C-4 explosive to throw into the water and detonate anything or anyone who might be under the water and sabotaging the bridge. As he struck the automatic lighter, setting off the time-delay fuse and detonation cord, and was preparing to throw the charge into the water, without warning, the charge prematurely exploded.

The blast shredded both of Mick's arms and his neck. The squad leader, who was fifty feet away, was injured by the bones from Mick's arms. Mick never lost consciousness during the whole event, even though the skin on his neck, chest, and face had been severely opened up. Was the life of this Marine over? No, Mick went back to college, earned a master's degree in business, and became vice president of a little company called IBM. Yet, as he worked closely with generals, CEOs, and even the President of the United States, he could not reconcile who he was as a private in Vietnam with who he was as an executive with IBM. It was a problem many veterans would have.

After a short greeting and "Welcome Homes," the party retired to the private residence of Daniel Albert Lane and his family. There was a cake with an American flag on it and the words "Welcome Home" printed smartly beneath the flag. Polaroid pictures were taken, which showed Christina and Damon sitting beside each other on the couch as the party continued. Here were two people sitting together for the first time in months. Christina was very happy, and it showed. Damon was also happy and very glad to have been home. He had survived the year without much more than a scratch. Yet the picture on the Polaroid showed two truths.: a very happy and joyful Christina and her Marine, biting his nails with a thousand-yard stare on his face. He knew he was home, but had no idea where he was.

In a few days, Damon went to the unemployment office and talked to the VA representative there. The man was very helpful and gave Damon some forms to fill out to have his teeth fixed and brought up to the standard of care, since Vietnam was actually very hard on their teeth. Damon's visits to a dentist in Vietnam had been few and far between, but that's the way it had been.

The VA rep said, "Go next door to the unemployment office and sign up for unemployment because there were no jobs in Yakima."

Damon took the forms, left the office without turning them in, and found a job. Damon's new job did not pay a lot, but he and Christina were on their way with their new life.

## *Heart Shot Fifteen*

*Damon had often wondered if man was designed to be ripped away from family, friends, and the land he was raised in. Then be placed in a foreign war zone? He often doubted they should have been. But the reality was there would always be turmoil and always be bad guys who needed to be reined in. Damon Lee Lane had always been an easy-going, melancholy type of a person, but he was not a wimp. He had volunteered to serve his country and had volunteered for the United States Marine Corps. Love of country was something that his parents had always taught him. Love God, your country, and treat others the way you would want to be treated. Damon had also been taught a strong work ethic, which proved to work over and over again in his life. To that end, he was very grateful to his parents and figured these pillars in his life was part of what brought him back safely.*

*Yet, in Damon's heart, he had a feeling something was still amiss. Something was still unsolved, such as the feeling of tension in his stomach that would not let up. He began to suspect the adrenaline rush he had been on his whole tour of duty was still involved. Adrenaline won't let you stop or slow down. It was necessary for Damon to keep moving and pushing forward with his life. Slowing down, stopping, or going backward was not an option.*

*The problem was, a year on adrenaline affects more than just the flight or fight response. Cortisone, cortisol, and adrenaline produced by the adrenal glands would affect their brains and several other organs in their bodies. It would be years before the effects of stress would become known. Then the term "post-traumatic stress" would blossom into public knowledge and the follow up post-traumatic stress syndrome and disorder would come to light.*

*Damon would now fight alone and in silence because nobody could possibly understand what he had been through and where he had been. What was he supposed to do when he was hurting on the inside but laughing out loud on the outside? Should he just pretend and go on? After all, he hadn't been wounded on the outside and was glad to be home. Many veterans developed a drinking problem when they returned because it numbed the pain, if even for a short time.*

# Chapter Sixteen

## *When the War is Over and Johnny Comes Marching Home*

DAMON HAD BEEN a civilian for several months and was trying to fit into a society that continued to live as if nothing had happened the last year or so. He tried to pick up where he left off and get on with his life. His war was over … but was it really? Some say, "When the war is over, a new one begins."

Damon had made it a point to leave it all behind him and move into the dream life that he had fantasized about while in Vietnam. One day, Damon was well on his way to work for the 12 to 9 p.m. shift at the local hardware store. He was driving down River Road, but didn't know it was Veterans Day and there was a parade downtown. Also unknown to him was that a Phantom jet flyby was scheduled for just after 11 a.m. that morning.

The jet was making its final approach to buzz Yakima Avenue, and it happened to fly just over Damon's car. The next thing he knew, he was on the floorboard of his 1966 Dodge Dart and ducking for cover. In just a millisecond, Damon realized he was driving and quickly pulled himself back into the driver's seat. He was amazed that his car had continued down River Road without veering to the right or left. Damon thought to himself how ridiculous his reaction was. He hadn't been in combat for at least ten months.

Other things seemed to bother Damon, too. Things like grassy fields that had tree lines around them. Helicopters that flew overhead on their way to the Yakima Firing Center, the military base just north of town. He couldn't easily accept overbearing people, so he avoided them like the plague. He dismissed the fact that he could not sleep all night and thought it was because he had been gone so long. Or perhaps it had been because he didn't sleep too much in 'Nam and he needed to just catch up.

Anger, well, Damon really didn't think he had a problem with anger except when the United States left Vietnam to its demise and Da Nang fell to the communists. Damon was very upset. How could so much be asked of his Marines, then in the stroke of pen, all was given over to the communists? This was too much for Daman's mind to handle. When he heard on television the machine guns firing and enemy troops taking over Da Nang, Damon retrieved all the maps and other things he had brought home from the war, piled them in his driveway, and set them on fire! No anger problem here! Damon sensed that the war was never going to really be over for him. It did not have an end, but it lived on in the minds and hearts of those who fought. It would surely live on in the hearts of those who had lost at war—the moms and dads, the wives and children of men who had paid the last full measure of devotion.

Yes, the war lived on. As Damon matured and developed a desire to better himself, two attitudes brewed within him. He had a desire to improve his life through college and job improvement, yet his stress jar had never been emptied or diminished. Who knew at this time of his life that the adrenaline constantly working in his system would lead to imbalanced cortisol levels and affect almost every area of his life? The combat stress was slowly leading to a malady called post-traumatic stress and the disorder that would set in because of it. Yet Damon had the drive to succeed. Half drive to succeed, half post-traumatic stress disorder (PTSD) as it was later called, drove Damon to go to college and get a degree. It was only after his college time and degree that he began to figure out what was really going on.

One day, sitting in his office, he heard a strange but familiar voice on the answering machine. "Hey, Lane. This is Manni. Give me a call sometime." Shock set in. It was undeniably one of the guys with whom he had served in Vietnam. Damon called him back in a few days. How had Manni found him? Manni told him that he had Damon's mom's phone number in his 15-year-old photo album in Vietnam and called it. Mom gave him Damon's work number, and that's how it all happened.

Half shocked and numb and half excited to have contact with an old friend, Damon tucked his feelings away and tried to deal with all the emotions that were stirring inside of him.

Manni had said that the squad was finding each other one by one and they would like to keep in contact, except for the one or two that were full-blown alcoholics by then.

The next call came in a few weeks from Sgt Letty. Damon could only let the answering machine take the call. It was just too much. It would take time for him to process this new information and to consider getting together with these old friends, who he really did care for. The long and short of it was that Damon eventually called him back and they talked for several hours. Sgt Letty was a key player in encouraging Damon to get some help through the Veterans Administration for PTSD and other issues. In typical man and Marine fashion, it would take Damon several months to make the move to get any type of help. But that time would come, and it would have to be on Damon's terms. That's just how it had to be! An old song seemed to stick and replay in Damons mind! Over and over again.

When Johnny comes marching
home again,
Hurrah, hurrah!
We'll give him a hardy welcome then,
Hurrah, hurrah!
The men will cheer, the boys will shout,
The ladies, they will all turn out
And we'll all feel gay
When Johnny comes marching home.

The sound and the music faded off into the distant, and the whole idea of cheering and shouting cheers had only been a dream. There were no marching parades, no bands welcoming Veterans home; they just slid into home, safe at last. Very few Americans, if any, were anywhere near proud of the Veterans as perhaps they should have been.

Were liberal ideas really working on the mainstream of America? It seemed like they were. Damon wondered if the protesting and free love message with lots of drugs and anti-establishment propaganda were taking their toll. Why, even God had been thrown out of the school systems and America had become smarter than God. It appeared that America was losing its way. And men had given their lives to support a failing system of government.

Realizing once again that America was ungrateful, most men just went to work and pretended they were normal and things were alright. Some even became ashamed that they served in the military and tried to hide that fact by saying they had just been out of town for a while. Soon the Veterans were wearing their hair long and shaggy just like the protestors were. It was hard to tell them apart.

Even with the sadness of what was happening to the country, Damon Lee was not going to surrender to this mob of insanity. There always had been right and wrong, and he was certain drug-sniffing hippies protesting and dressing sloppy were not in the cards for him.

So, Damon kind of figured America had really changed since he had been away, but he also realized he had changed. Deep in his heart, he had changed. But what was it? What was the missing piece he sensed was missing?

By now, Damon realized that deep in his heart could be a complicated place. It had been a place of reason, a place of warning, and a place where peace is made—or not! Damon knew that some men never came to them-selves following traumatic events. Some did, but they usually didn't get there by themselves. This was Damon's story. He had gotten in touch with a group of guys called Point Man Ministries, which was a support group mainly for Vietnam veterans. Of course, Damon was at first in denial and didn't really need any help and was pretty sure the ones who did had gotten a hold of some had weed or something like that.

He had never been so wrong in all his life.

Quite by accident Damon made contact with a PTSD counselor at the local VA clinic. He had been there a week or two before to drop off a few boxes of cookies leftover from a youth event. When he left, he was shaking so bad he had trouble putting the keys in the ignition. Very soon, Damon returned to find out what was wrong. He walked into the center on his day off and just blurted out, "Do you guys test for PTSD here?"

The lady who greeted Damon was a few years older than him and looked like she could be his aunt. She said, "Yeah, we do that, but why don't we just come back to my office and talk?"

Well, Damon could do that.

Once inside this woman's office, Damon felt right at home. It had two walls full of Marine Corps memorabilia. "Were you in the Marines?" Damon asked as he looked for the nearest exit.

She shrugged and said, "No, I've never been in the service at all. I just like Marines!"

Damon knew he was in the right place, and through the next year and a half, he found out what PTSD was doing and began to manage its effects as well.

## Heart Shot Sixteen

*This heart shot was not an easy one, and it required paying close attention and actually doing something, not just talking about it! Oh, the talks weren't the hardest part. It was the opening up that had bothered Damon the most. Opening up to another person, a woman at that? Impossible because of Damon's preconceived ideas. He had built a wall up just to guard what was inside.*

*This lady, this counselor, slowly and gently eased his pain, and together they discovered a lot of hidden barriers that needed to be examined.*

*Damon finally realized that his PTSD did not need to be cured; that was only done by a miracle. But it could be managed, and that was the goal. Sometimes a heart shot was not always there to kill. Sometimes they were used to heal, to repair, and to set the whole person on the road to recovery. Who would have thought that talking and looking at a situation could make all the difference in the world? Damon had gained a whole new appreciation for professional counseling and his local Veterans center.*

# Chapter Seventeen

## *More Voices from the Past*

DAMON HAD ALREADY heard from Manni and could not believe it had actually happened. Manni was living in San Diego and it was hard to understand how someone could actually live that close to the Marine Corps boot camp and survive. A lot of things had happened over the years but Manni seemed to be the same as he was in Vietnam.

Second Platoon had a Marine who always came around and visited for a few minutes once they all got set in their foxholes late in the day. They all called him Chief. They knew his real name, but Chief worked for them and him. Damon thought he was Filipino but that didn't matter; Chief was a Marine, and a good one at that. They learned later that Chief rotated back to the States, and couldn't handle stateside duty, so he volunteered for a second tour of duty. He was killed during his second tour, in an accident no less. Some said it was a trucking accident. He was gone, and they didn't give Purple Hearts for accidents, which upset all the other platoon members who heard the news. Believe it or not, they got to meet Chief's sister twenty years later, because Manni had married her. She was a real sweetheart of a gal and proved to Manni that he had made a wise investment in marrying her.

Manni had a quick type of a talk and got somewhat excited when he was trying to explain something. Between that and his accent, he always gave everyone something to laugh about. Who would have thought that Manni would marry Chief's sister and the squad would hear the story of what happened to him. The memory of Chief lived on in Damon's heart. And of course, a smile was always generated when he thought of Manni.

Other smiles would come when Damon remembered the time when 2$^{nd}$ Squad needed another Marine to go out on patrol because they were short-handed. Wild Wit actually sold or rented Manni to Ski, who was the 2$^{nd}$ Squad leader so he would have the men he needed. That was funny then and it was still funny, every time the subject came up. Another small thing that would be remembered for a lifetime.

Soon there were other voices, Sgt Letty and Wild Wit heard the word about Damon. There was talk of a reunion in Las Vegas and soon it was on. The trip had been planned and planes landed from around the United States to see, perhaps for the last time, their combat buddies. The men were going to meet that evening for the first time at the coffee shop in their motel.

Damon carefully worked his way down to the coffee shop area and tried to scope it out before he fully committed to seeing guys he hadn't seen for thirty years. Strangely enough, the coffee shop was empty except for a group of older guys sitting in a booth. A few seconds later, Damon thought he recognized the tall one. Then, sure enough, it was them. They all looked different than when they last saw each other in 1969. But after a few reintroductions and a few minutes of time, it all began to come back to them. There was Wild Wit, Sgt Letty, WOP, Dizzy, Manni, and as the night progressed, the list grew.

The next few days were glorious ones. Dinners, gambling (which was a tradition in Vegas, of course), time to share together as a unit, and private times just to talk with each other. Some brought hats and shirts as gifts, some brought books to share, but mainly each man brought himself. That was enough. The stories that would be told that night about the lives of those men since Vietnam could have filled many a book of mystery, adventure, sorrow, and heartache. But these were Damon's brothers. Blood brothers, in fact. They were the few, the happy few, this band of brothers!

The Apostle Paul asked in his writings, "What can separate us from the love of God?" Damon thought and realized that nothing could separate these men from their bond together. Time, hardship, adversity, death? No, their bond would always live on. They didn't have to talk every day, once a month, or see each other ever again, but their bond remained true and strong. Perhaps there was more about love for your brothers, especially Veterans who have served together, that cannot be explained as much as they thought they could. Perhaps the Apostle Paul was right in his writings, as well as Jesus, who said, "Greater love hath no man this this, that a man lay down his life for his friends!" (John 15:13). Damon kind of thought in his younger years that the Bible was old fashioned and for "churchy" type people but some of the wisdom in its contents had surely been played out on the battlefield.

Oddly enough, voices a little closer to home began to get into the action. Damon's original boot camp platoon began to get in touch with each other and began to have regular reunions in Washington State. Trips to the Marine Corps recruit depot and local outings were planned and executed. There was a brotherhood there also, but not one quite as strong like the bond of 1st Squad, 1st Platoon, Hotel Company.

Many men from the boot camp platoon did, however, serve with the 26th Marine Regiment in Vietnam. Second Battalion, 26th Marine Regiment had become known as the Nomads because they did not have a regular base to operate from, but assaulted off Navy ships when things hit the fan. Not having a home base was alright with them, because home to them was somewhere back in the States.

During one of these boot camp reunions, LCpl Damon heard from one of his boot camp buddies about how he got out of Vietnam early. He was serving with 3rd Battalion, 26th Marine Regiment, another regimental battalion that worked with 2nd Battalion, 26th Marine Regiment in the greater scheme of things. He also was an Italian, but we just called him Davey.

Davey was under fire from an NVA force and his unit was getting small arms and mortar fire. As he got back from checking on a friend who had almost been blasted away by a mortar round but wasn't actually even injured, an 81-mm mortar landed right in front of Davey. The blast knocked him into the foxhole, and he felt like a baseball bat had struck him in his face. Yet he wasn't in pain.

Funny thing, he wasn't in his body, either. He looked down, and he saw his body lying in the foxhole and a corpsman frantically working on him before giving up and leaving. Davey was suspended about thirty feet above his body. He wondered what had happened. *I think I'm dead. What do I do now?* He looked above himself and saw two shiny little twinkly lights coming down from above, twinkling like they were talking to each other. *Well, these must be angels, and they're coming to get me*, which was odd for him because he had only gone to church maybe twice a year unless he had something else to do. Within a few seconds, the lights soon stopped descending, twinkled to each other a couple more times. then left. Davey told Damon, "When they left, I had felt all alone in the universe and I knew I was really screwed."

Suddenly, he was back in his body, and the corpsman, who was leaving, turned white as a ghost when he saw Davey get out of the foxhole and begin walking toward him. The long and short of it was that Davey got an early out from 'Nam, but spent many months in a hospital in Guam. His eye was almost removed by his doctors because of the damage, but they put it back in and on a wait and see basis. Davey's eye recovered, and the stitches in his face could barely be seen after they had healed. Also, Davey later said, "I can see better out of the injured eye than I can my good eye."

It would take a couple more years before Davey got a real clear understanding of the events that day. The lights that twinkled, the feeling of being alone after they left, and the feeling that he was screwed all came into focus a few years later. But that is Davey's story to tell. And, yes, he has written a book about it called *Twice Dead Now I Live*.

## *Heart Shot Seventeen*

*Damon had struggled when hearing the voices of the Veterans with whom he had served. Wartime and trauma had left a lot of loose ends. Sometimes, he thought it better to leave the ends loose and try not to tie them together again. But all things happen for a purpose, and the reunion with 1st Squad, 1st Platoon and Platoon 3041 from boot camp had surely been meant to be.*

*Heart shots, like voices from the past, had been a Godsend. Knowing your buddies were still around, out there living their lives, had encouraged Damon. One movie about Vietnam, Platoon, had a line that said, "The war is over for me now, but it will always there the rest of my days. ... those of us who did make it have an obligation to build again, to teach others what we know, and to try with what's left of our lives to find a goodness and a meaning to this life." Those were wise words, in Damon's opinion. And who knew that somehow all things could work together to make one whole again. Even heart shots from the past.*

# Chapter Eighteen

## *Miracles Worth Waiting For*

ONE OF THE biggest questions that crossed almost anyone's mind was the question of miracles. How did some Veterans make it back, while others did not? Were they just lucky? Or was there a reason, like some were better at the game of war? Or was it a toss of the dice? Damon had these questions from time to time. They didn't always need to be answered, but they were always there. For him, it was personal. He knew it would be cruel to try to give quick, not well-thought-through answers to these questions, especially to the family that had lost the loved one. So, this type of question would need to be answered for oneself, if answered at all.

The heroic medics—or corpsman, as they were called in the Navy/Marines—had done an excellent job of patching up the wounded and getting them transported to a nearby aid station. So, had they been part of some miracle? Well, Damon did not let this go idly. He had learned that a miracle could be defined as "a surprising and welcome event that is not explicable by natural or scientific laws and is therefore considered to be the work of a divine agency."

So, had a medic putting on a bandage, stopping the bleeding, and transporting the wounded, been a miracle? By definition, no. It could be scientifically explained. However, the wounded man being able to survive his wounds could be designated a miracle when others with the same type of wounds had died. In other words, there is more to living than plugging up wounds. The innate born will of survival could be greater in one than the other. Or, had there been divine intervention for this person through a thing called prayer? And could the prayer have been made thousands of miles away? In Damon's opinion, the answer was yes. He had experienced at least four miracles while he was in Vietnam.

The first was the ability of anyone to survive the savagery of war. The living conditions alone were enough to strangle the life out of someone, never mind the ever-present enemy. Damon had thought many times about this and then realized that if it were truly a miracle, then why did some very good men not make it? He knew a pastor's son who did not survive Vietnam, and if we're talking miracles, shouldn't he have been one? The other question was that how would it make those who have lost someone feel if God did not protect their loved ones but protected others? Good questions. But then it becomes very easy to put oneself in place of God with these questions. There were just some things that had to be left in God's hands and not ours. Again, Damon knew it had been a miracle he had made it home.

The second miracle was the night Damon had spotted the patrol on the other side of the creek, heading to the same footbridge to set up ambushes. With his melancholy personality, he had always kept things straight; it was part of his nature. That night, he felt it was divine intervention that made him aware of the column of men moving through the darkness. It had been so dark, nobody could have possibly seen the other men. He recalled when Wit looked, he didn't see them at first, either. But then he did. The events that followed could have taken the lives of many a man, yet they lived.

The third miracle was when the ARVNs opened up on their squad after the night ambush. The bullets had flown and zoomed by each man, yet no one got hurt. Damon also recalled how once in the bush he was opened up on by a sniper using automatic fire as Damon was doing his daily head call. He had immediately hit the ground, and the bullets, which had tracer rounds in them, with quick flashes of light, zipped through the grass, missing his head by just inches. Had he been lucky? Was it just not his time to go? Who could say? Damon truly believed it was an act of God. Somewhere, the message got through and a divine presence was watching over them!

The fourth and final miracle that Damon experienced was long after he had returned home. Damon had worked for a hardware store for a couple of years after 'Nam. Then for the Toyota Motor Company for eight and a half years. Damon had always wanted to do more with his life and decided to go to chiropractic college in South Carolina. After years of school, examinations, and state boards, he set up his chiropractic practice in Yakima, WA, and met a lot of very nice patients, and always treated them as he would like to be treated.

After years in practice, there still was something Damon needed to do. He had put it off for years, but it was always there in his mind. He needed to write LCpl Michaels' parents, the man who had replaced him in Vietnam and was later killed. Damon had been going to the VA in Yakima for help with resolution for some issues he was dealing with, and the counselor there was very helpful. She helped Damon locate his replacement's parents, who lived in Mandon, SD.

Damon carefully worded the letter, typed it so they could read it, double-checked everything to make sure it was what he wanted to say, and placed it on his desk at work for another month. One more month to work up the courage to mail it.

One day, after Damon arrived at his office, he decided he would mail it that day, so he put the letter in the outgoing mail. That was the day, the day he had put off for so long. He wasn't sure why he wanted to write to them, but he knew he wanted to ease their pain, if only for just a little. Damon thought it might help Michaels' folks to know that others cared about the trouble they had gone through and that their loved one would always be remembered. Perhaps the small token of a letter could be an oil of healing as well.

Later that morning, a patient came in for a chiropractic tune up. She said they were going on a trip to South Dakota that afternoon and wanted to feel her best for the trip. She was in her eighties and had been a patient for years.

Damon had asked her, "Where in South Dakota are you going?"

"Mandon," she replied, "Mandon, South Dakota."

Damon, Dr. Damon by now, was shocked. He told her the whole story about Vietnam, how Michaels died, and that for thirty years he had wanted to write his parents. And that just that day, he had put the letter in the outbox to mail.

This very sweet lady said, "Would you like me to hand-deliver it?" Damon could not believe what was happening. It would be the perfect plan, a hand-delivered letter by good Christian people who he knew were solid people, and who cared for others. This was the fourth miracle. Damon retrieved the letter from the outbox and placed it into the hands of this angel of a person.

He was quite content that this was more than a letter, it was a mission, and it had God's hand all over it. A month later, when the couple returned from their motor home adventure, they came into the office and told the whole story. First, they said that Michaels' parents were very glad that someone remembered their son, second that the letter and personal visit was very much appreciated. The lady who visited them had taken pictures of Michaels' mom and dad, his picture on their wall of him in his Marine dress blues, as well as a picture of his Bronze Star and Purple Heart, for his wounds and death. The patient had also made copies for Dr. Damon to keep.

The two elderly couples had such a wonderful time visiting, and the last miracle of the visit was that they found out they were related to each other. They were distant cousins who had not known each other until they began to visit and talk. Michaels' mom and dad were elderly by then, and Damon heard that they had passed on a few years afterwards. Damon, to this day, believes that this mission of mercy was orchestrated or at least blessed by the unseen power who cares and watches over us all. Luck? Chance? He didn't think so!

## *Heart Shot Eighteen*

*By definition, miracles can be claimed for a lot of things. The thing just can't be explained by science or natural laws. It could be easily argued that things just happened, and yes, they did! Yet Damon really wondered how men could go through combat like they did, come home, and live for years and years without some guiding force helping them. Damon had always thought there was an unseen force active in all our lives. The question was not if He was there, but rather why do some know this and others not? Damon had always thought it was a good question and worth some time pondering.*

*In Damon's mind, the letter to Michaels' folks could have been sent earlier, but perhaps there was a reason for the long delay. How it all worked out was miraculous. It could not have been planned that way by humans. Not the way it worked out.*

*Damon would be thankful every day of his life to have survived the war. Even the new war that began in his heart and those of every Vietnam combat Veteran. Other people had suffered trauma, and that's not new. But post-traumatic stress from war had its own special way of affecting a person and has its own way to be treated. Most VA Counselors and Psychologist say it never goes away, but it could be managed in such a way that Veterans' lives could be lived without the effects of the trauma that rendered havoc on their closest family members and society, in general. This is not to mention the part inside of the heart that was in need of rest.*

*For Damon, the nightmares, the false sense that someone was out to get him, the sleepless nights, and some flash-backs and intrusive thoughts had, for the most part, been put to rest. His most recurring dream was that he was being called back to Vietnam by the Marine Corps. This had always caused panic because one tour of duty was all he had ever wanted.*

*The last type of dream like this happened early in the morning hours. He had been called back to the Corps and was being sent straight to Vietnam. He realized he was in San Francisco and had gotten on the trolley car with the other Marines heading for the airplane to take them back to Vietnam. As Damon looked at the Marines in all their combat gear, he noticed he had on his three-piece suit with his silver pocket watch attached to his vest. He thought, I'm not dressed to go back to Vietnam, and he slowly got off the trolly and walked away. This was his last dream ever, about going back to Vietnam.*

# Chapter Nineteen

## Life After War & Picking Up the Pieces

DAMON HAD GONE to the VA and received help from a PTSD counselor. It had been the most humbling experience he ever had, yet it was the wisest. He had been carrying stuff around and could not fix it on his own. Damon had also joined a group called Point Man Ministries, which was a support group and an information source for Veterans struggling in relationships. Between the two, he had begun to feel his life was getting back on track.

The counseling sessions and Point Man information taught him several things about what happens after the war is over. With PTSD, Veterans, both men or women, could experience the following.

### Intrusive Thoughts and Flashbacks

The Veteran thinks about the war much of the time. Sometimes, this involves thinking about how a certain action could have been done differently, and many times it includes replaying the event and searching for alternative outcomes. The flashbacks would be where the Veteran would actually be transported back to the event in their mind. These flashbacks were more than just thoughts. For a few seconds the event was so real, it was like the Veteran was "there" again!

## Isolation

They feel the need to isolate themselves from family members emotionally, and sometimes geographically. The Veteran often fantasizes about becoming a hermit and not having to deal with stuff!

## Emotional Numbing

The Veteran fears losing control ... fears not keeping their act together, and fears that someone will die because they lose control. They are sure that if they ever start crying, they might not stop. They feel emotional expression is a weakness. They can't really experience true emotions other than anger and any other activity that will provide them an adrenaline rush!

## Depression

The Veteran usually has low self-esteem and lacks energy or desire to accomplish tasks and responsibilities. They have suicidal thoughts and think people would be better off if they weren't there. They can be in a bad mood most of the time and experience self-pity very often. They often blame others for their problems.

## Outward Anger

They have quiet, masked rage, which is frightening to the Veteran and others near them. They may throw and break things when upset. They also easily lose control and spill their attitude over to their family.

## Substance Abuse

The Veteran uses alcohol or drugs too much and too often to diminish the pain. They make things happen to cause excitement, such as a single-car accident, or upsets their spouse so there will be an argument; therefore, they get a new high off adrenaline. Adrenaline is a drug.

## Guilt

They experience survivor's guilt, for surviving when others died around them. "If only I ..." The unanswered question of why they made it when others didn't plays daily in their mind.

## Stress

The Veteran feels conditional suspense, does not trust others. They never really relax. Their stress jar is full, all the way to the top! Any new stress the Veteran experiences causes a hyper response, one that is usually inappropriate.

## Denial

They are unable to admit that they have any of the above symptoms of PTSD. The Veteran is unwilling to seek help and says, "Things are OK! I can take care of it myself!"

This had not been an exhaustive list of symptoms, but for many it hit the nail on the head. It was the first awareness that something was not quite right. Most Veterans, Damon included, would double-check all the doors at night to make sure they were locked. He had uneasy feelings when someone criticized him and struggled hard at accepting change. What really was a reality for Veterans was their struggle accepting orders and others in authority. They also felt very uneasy in groups of people and did not like crowds. They liked people to be spread out and to not get into groups. And, somehow, they developed a hypersensitivity to injustice. Sometimes the Veteran could be having a good day, but that would change suddenly when any of the following occurred: the smell of urine, diesel fuel, or ethnic food, especially Chinese; the sounds of helicopters, of a car backfiring, or of someone walking up behind them quickly; environmental challenges, like a rainy and gloomy cloud-covered day; and flat ground covered with short grass with tree lines surrounding the area. Things like Fourth of July celebrations were often out of the question.

At one Point Man conference, all the Veterans set in the back of the auditorium and very close to the exits on the first day. They wanted to make sure they could get out quickly if they were ambushed by Point Man! Also, they wanted to be in the back row so no one could sit behind them. They were reminded that they were among friends, and they had their backs. With some coaching, the Veterans moved forward just a little, and the conference turned out to be life-changing for most of them.

The symptoms of PTSD that Damon had learned about were characteristic of combat Veterans. They were not abnormal, and they were in themselves a normal reaction to abnormal circumstances. They were not excuses for bad behavior for the Veteran. But it did give them and their families the knowledge that none of them were alone when the symptoms of PTSD attacked. In previous wars, the symptoms had different names, but the effects were the same.

Many Veterans clubs flourished after World War II because they provided comradery to the Veteran. Plus, after a few drinks of alcohol, things seemed to settle down. Unfortunately, the alcohol had only numbed them more, and many Veterans became full-blown alcoholics. They had changed from an addiction to adrenaline to an addiction to alcohol. Damon made these observations, which were stored away for a better time, when they could be processed.

Their family would ask them, "Where have you been the last four hours?" Many Veterans would say, "Oh, I was at the church, talking to the preacher (bartender), church people were there (other drinkers), and the spirit (booze) was flowing freely." This was more of a joke than anything. It reminded Damon of the Veterans who went to war and didn't want anyone to know that they had gone. When some asked where they had been, many would say, "Oh, I've been out of town!"

To Damon, it seemed that when people were hurt, they could hurt others. This is the law of society and American society has done a very poor job of caring for one another. With the drug addictions, many addicts had learned from their parents about drugs. For sure, most learned how to drink that way. Yet they've all made excuses and said it was all right to do what they wanted, even at the expense of family. And so the dysfunction was passed on from one generation to the next. The local mission that was in Damon's town reported that 93 percent of homeless people had been severely hurt or abused, usually by a family member or someone they knew. The cycle continued, and everybody wondered, what could be done?

One mother had been away for three days on a drug binge, leaving her three kids at home to fend for themselves. When she returned home and found the twelve-year-old son, the oldest, had taken care of the family in her absence, she taught him how to use meth as a reward. This was the terrible type of dysfunction that was running rampant in America.

As chaplain of the local Marine Corps League in his hometown, Damon thought long and hard about this. With the local Point Man group, they took to the streets and missions, looking for Veterans who wanted a hand up. Many have been helped, and two very great guys joined Point Man and got off the streets. They improved, got jobs, one of them got married, and both had their own homes. Street living had taken its toll, and they have both passed on now, but before they died, they got a handle on their problems, they got a handle on their PTSD symptoms, and they got a handle on life. How had this been possible? All they had really needed was for someone to care about them. Someone who had traveled their road before. Someone to offer them guidance without them feeling like they were receiving new orders.

One of the men's name was Robert E. Webb. Everyone called him "Web E." He kind of liked that. When Damon first met him at a local mission, Damon had recognized a Vietnam flag bumper sticker on a truck outside. Damon asked, in a little elevated voice because the service at the mission hadn't started yet, "Anybody know whose little blue truck is out in front of the mission?"

A rather large barrel-chested, hard-looking man stood, turned toward Damon, and growled, "It's mine. What the hell is it to ya?"

Well, Damon knew by now his roughness was only a smokescreen. He walked over to old Web E., shook his hand, gave him a hug, and said, "Welcome home, brother!"

Damon invited him to come to a Point Man meeting, but Web E. declined because it would be in the evening and he needed to be there at the mission because it was his only chance to have a meal. Damon told him that if he wanted to come to Point Man, a meal would be provided. It just so happened that Damon had prepared to talk that night about PTSD and its effects on combat Veterans. After the short talk and the men were filing into the Dining Hall, Damon noticed the man last in line was old Web E. He stopped, shook Damon's hand, and said, "Thank you for the information. I'd never heard of that before. Oh, and when is that meeting again?"

Old Web E. started coming to the meetings and in a short time began to release some really hard, pent-up anger! On the way to a Point Man conference, old Web E. rode in Damon's car in the passenger seat. Over the course of five hours, Damon heard the whole story of what had happened to Web E. He had gotten married in Colorado right after Vietnam. All seemed well, but it seemed his wife would criticize him on just about everything. Web E. could live with that, but soon after their two girls were born, the criticizing increased, along with his sister and mother-in-law joining in. That did not go well.

Soon, he didn't know what to do. His job at the Coors Bottling Company ended abruptly, and all hell broke loose when he lost this good paying job! Now he was looked upon as a loser and was further railed upon by his wife, her mother, and his sister in law. Web E.'s fuse was lit, burning rapidly, and about to cause a very large explosion!

He knew what he had been capable of in Vietnam. He didn't want to be involved in that type of score-settling again. So, he did the next best thing in his mind. Instead of fighting, he ran. The very next day after the kids were in school and his wife was at work, he wrote a letter, placed it on the kitchen table, went to the local bus depot and left … never to return! He blamed it all on his wife, Maria.

This had been a tragedy, yet it was a tragedy that was played out across the USA many times a day, many times a week, many times a month. Lives shattered, and for what? Damon had a hard time believing that one woman could be that bad. Upon further talking with Web E. and providing him with some skills to think properly, respond appropriately and learn fine art of forgiveness, Web E. began to realize he had responded inappropriately to an abnormal situation. Without patience and proper thinking, many would have done the same thing! Web E. had been a victim of his own inner peace or lack of it, and became another victim of PTSD. Damon remembered the symptoms of PTSD and realized Web E. had all of them.

However, help was on the way, and Point Man was able to come alongside and help him. Knowing the heart of mankind and their nature, though, they all realized the changes going on inside of Web E. would have to come from a higher power, birthed from God and dispersed through the loving care of a few fellow Veterans who had been there before.

On another note, when Web. E. passed away, a short slide show was mailed to the ex-wife just as a thoughtful gesture. She called the church after getting it and wanted Point Man's phone number. Damon told the pastor, "I don't want to talk to her, but she can email me!"

The email went kind of like this: I want the flag, I want his truck, and I want any money he had left. She'd had no contact with him and kept his two daughters away except for maybe one time in a thirty-year span.

Damon kindly said, "The flag went to the next of kin at the funeral, and his money and truck also went to his sister to pay for part of the funeral. However, if you guys would like to help pay for the funeral, then we can see how much is left after that!" Damon did not hear from her again and he realized that Web E.'s summation of what he had gone through with this woman was more accurate than anybody had known.

Web. E was memorialized and received full military honors at his funeral. Damon was honored when he was asked to be part of this Army guy's funeral. His ceremony was held at the West Valley Missionary Church, a place Web E. had grown to love, and where they loved him.

Point Man also helped his surviving sister move and clean out his apartment and settle his affairs. That was what Veterans do for each other. After all, was that not the meaning of Semper Fidelis (Always Faithful), the Marine Corps' motto?

## *Heart Shot Nineteen*

*Damon had never cared for the idea of PTSD and had done the best he could without help. He had struggled a long time all by himself, but with family and friends around most of the time. Damon learned that PTSD should never have be taken lightly. He had done so, and it cost him dearly.*

*The road for Damon Lee Lane had been long and hard. Yet a few years after Vietnam, he made peace with God and his relationship was restored. It wasn't a cakewalk after that, either. But through the pain and entanglements of problems that were associated with PTSD, he had come out a better man. Damon's greatest satisfactions in life had become to help other Veterans off the bottom of society and life and so they could live again.*

# Chapter Twenty

## *Striking Your Last Match*
## *An Essay from the Author*

I HOPE YOU have been able to follow the story of Damon, who was pictured as a tender-hearted young man turned Marine. I wanted to paint a picture of what can happen when anyone is traumatized. Have you ever seen a movie where people are freezing and they have one match left? Their life depends on whether the last match lights or goes out. These movies have always been scary for me. Movies where scuba divers go into unmarked underwater caves without ropes and markers also send my adrenaline climbing. These situations would carry trauma of their own. I think it is good for us all to ask ourselves, "Have I been traumatized in any way?" If you haven't, then you are one of the few. Good for you. But if you have been and feel like somehow you are living on the edge with nowhere to go, there's hope.

One of the characteristics of post-war Veterans who developed PTSD was that they never got used to not having an adrenaline experience. Many would join biker clubs to get the rush of driving fast on their motorcycle. This had a lot of good effects by giving the Veteran a sense of control, a sense of speed, and of course a rush. It kind of felt good to get a rush once in a while. Many single-car accidents by Veterans were from driving too fast or carelessly to obtain some sort of adrenaline rush so they could feel normal again. Usually, if a bar was frequented and too much alcohol was consumed, it was easy for the Veteran to pick a fight with someone else, just for the rush. With a chip on their shoulder, it wouldn't take much for anything to set them off into a rage of swearing and fighting.

This activity doesn't only happen to combat Veterans. Many people who have experienced trauma act the same way. Perhaps the intensity is less, but many drive their cars around endlessly, speeding, not paying attention, and often not stopping at stop signs. This type of activity allows them to feel like they are normal because an adrenaline surge takes place when they live on the edge. And even though the trauma they experienced was bad, it gave them an adrenaline rush—something to which many were addicted.

Sometimes, it takes years for traumatized people to figure it all out. Some never do. Some self-medicate with alcohol, drugs, or even tobacco. All this self-medication does is help cover up the injury and pain, but it may buy them a little more time to figure it all out. I remember the parable about a young man who demanded his father give him his inheritance early. He then went into another country where he lived it up, foolishly spending his money on riotous living. When his money was gone, so were his friends. He became a servant and fed pigs so he would have something to eat. Finally, when it came to him what he had done, he realized how self-centered and selfish he had been. The teller of the parable said, "When he came to himself, he went back to his father's house and repented." He was accepted back into the family by his father, whose heart had been yearning to see his son again.

One of the greatest things that helped me through my time with PTSD was the truth. I found out that there was hope and that I wasn't even supposed to go it alone. Yet most of us like to ignore the help that's available, for several reasons. I personally didn't want anything to do with the government once I got out of the service. Not being wounded in combat, I also figured the VA was for those guys who had arms and legs missing. What I didn't know was that I also had been wounded—a wound of the heart and soul that wasn't getting any better on its own. Years later, I came to myself, so to speak. I realized that I did need help. That was when I became real to myself. Someone once said, "To thine own self be true." There has never been a more correct statement than that.

This part of the book may help you realize that perhaps you have not been true to yourself. Instead of honestly looking at what you've been through or what trauma you have experienced, you self-medicated or just kept on trying to make it on your own. The other erroneous way people deal with their problems is to keep hurting others. In some twisted way, this makes the traumatized person at least feel something. Emotional numbing, where you need a traumatic event to feel something, is not a good thing. Racing a car, dangerously riding a motorcycle, or even fighting or abusing someone else just to feel something can never be right. Yet it happens all the time. Hurting people hurt people. Where will the cycle stop, if not with us?

Getting help usually is something you have to want to do yourself. Sometimes a family counselor will suggest help for the Veteran, but usually their life will dwindle away until they have no choice. Get help, or run. Then there are times where a judge will order counseling or that the Veteran be locked up. Locking them up does not solve any problems for the Veteran, but it may save a family some trouble.

Wouldn't it be much better if the traumatized person could recognize their dilemma and take the steps necessary to correct it?

There are also times when a traumatized person only hurts themselves. They go on a destructive downwards spiral and are stuck in the trauma of the past. Many of these people will talk about problems, but the blame is usually put all on someone else, and they do not consider themselves part of the problem. They tell and retell the incident until they wear out their willing listener. With that bridge burned, they move on to someone else, while further hurting themselves because nothing is being accomplished. This is perhaps one of the saddest situations because until we "come to our self," no progress will be made.

As chaplain of the Marine Corps League and the outpost leader for Point Man, I have seen all these cases. It seemed like the ones who could move forward weren't the ones that knew it all. It wasn't the ones who thought they had all the answers. It was simply those who were willing to admit they did have a problem, and were willing to do something about it. These were the ones who began to enjoy life and moved further away from the trauma that happened so long ago. I have never liked the word "denial." Yet many people who were in it, are not aware of their own problems and have been tagged with it. They suffer alone, mainly because if they can't see the problem, then what is there to fix? An even better word—although, at first glance, it seems crueler—is ignorance. This simply means that they ignore the problem, hoping it will go away or that it wasn't really that big of a deal to begin with. Choosing to ignore that they are hurting themselves or others by not taking a good look at themselves is dangerous. In the medical field, one of the statements heard from patients all the time was, "I thought it would go away."

Most of us, when we break our arm, would not hesitate to go to the doctor for repair. Yet we become squeamish and unsettled when we think about getting some help with our heart, as if all heart shots are painful. Some are really meant to heal. Heart or soul repair does not always have to hurt, but you must be brave.

Perhaps you have been given one last match to light your way. Are you willing to strike it and let the embers break into a flame to guide your way and save your life now and for eternity? Your road may have been longer and harder than Damon's. I suspect it has been. Then you may need some help in fanning your last match into a flame that can last forever.

So, if God was watching over us in Vietnam, how come He didn't seem that close and very personal? As a chaplain for the Marine Corps League, I have come to realize that it was not God that had a problem with communication, it was us. I also realize that God did want a relationship, and has been reaching out to us and has had an eye on us, our whole life. I also realized that God does not have just one denomination of believers. He loves everybody and wants a relationship with us all. Protestant, Jew, Gentile, Catholic, even the atheist. The list goes on.

There was, though, a problem. We had been separated from God because of sin, and even not so much ours, but original sin with Adam and Eve. As Veterans, the enemy of our soul takes advantage of our misfortune of being traumatized, and we get caught up in a world of problems, feeling like nobody cares and there is no way out. Our senses become numb to the very idea that God even exists, and we become trapped in a booby trap of troubles.

This problem of entrapment in problems, PTSD, or even original sin, was solved by God's plan over two thousand years ago. God loved mankind so much and wanted a relationship with us so much, He gave His only Son to be a sacrifice for us. To pay the penalty for sin. Once paid, we have relationship with Him. We have guidance through Him, and we have a promise of eternal life with Him when we leave earth. Remember my friend Davey, from 3/26, who actually died in Vietnam and came back alive? He said, "When the two talking and twinkling lights were coming down to get me but stopped, talked then left? I felt all alone." That is how we are, alone. God seems at a distance, yet He sent his Son that whosoever would believe in Him would have everlasting life.

My friend who died and came back alive on the battlefield, came to understand years later what God had done for him. He became a minister and although now retired, traveled to Africa for a short time, trying to help youth understand who God is and what He has done.

My prayer for you, a Veteran, or any other person reading this book, is that you allow God into your life if you haven't already. God comes alongside when we ask Him to. With your last match in hand, the below prayer may help.

## *The Final Heart Shot*

*A simple prayer can usher you into the presence of God. It can go like this:*

*Dear God, I know you watched over me in Vietnam (or during any other trauma). I know that you want a relationship with me. I know that I have sinned just like everybody else. But I repent of any wrongdoing, and I accept a full pardon from you because of what Jesus did. I will not doubt you any longer.*

*Please come into my heart. I pray this in Jesus' name ... Amen.*

*The next step could be to read from the Bible for spiritual strength. If you are unfamiliar with the Bible and where to start reading, I suggest the Gospel of John as the place to start. John talks about a lot of things to get one started on a new spiritual journey. If the Bible has been boring for you in the past, perhaps you will find new meaning from it after you prayed the above prayer. If you did pray, you are now a child of God, and what many people call born again. You are on your way to heaven. God will reveal Himself to you like never before!*

My hope is that you didn't mind Damon and I walking point for you through this book. I was uncertain and didn't really know if I could write it, or even if I had the guts to. It was not an easy thing for me to do.

But here it is! Just one more mission—the last chapter, so to speak—and it will be over.

# Chapter Twenty-One

## *Where and How to Get Help*

WHEN I FIRST set out to start this book a year ago, I was on my way to California for our granddaughter's graduation from Azusa Pacific University. I thought writing would be a good distraction for me since I didn't really like to fly. Since then, I have gotten over my fear of flying and replaced it with the fear of crashing. Pretty much the same thing, but knowing your fears helps to solve them. It was kind of like getting the courage to attempt to write this book. The hours spent on working to that end were priceless, yet hard. If you have had the courage to finish reading this book, from my heart, thank you, and I hope it went well for you.

If you are a Veteran and still have unanswered questions about your war experiences or need help with counseling, please contact your local Veterans center. They have tons of information and help just waiting for your call. If you don't want to go there alone, be brave, ask a friend to go with you.

If you have served in the military, war or peacetime and are interested in Point Man International Ministries, their web page is: https://www.pmim.org/. Follow the links to find the nearest outpost to you. There is a lifeline number to talk to someone if you are in stress: 1-800-877-VETS. Point Man's International Headquarters is now in Minco, OK.

If you are not a Veteran and have finished this book and realize that God has been watching over you and would like further help, please seek out a local church. Most are full of loving Christian people who are on a spiritual journey and support each other to that end. Semper Fidelis!

# The End

Printed in Canada